BODIES BODIES

TRUE DREAMS OF WICHITA

SEAN MACKAAY

For Theo and Alison

BRENDAN
ALBERT
HOWARD

A SEA of eyes stared out at David. Half in shadow from the bright lecture hall lights blasting his eyes. He swallowed. He hated this moment. Every semester. An uncertain mass of students waiting, expectant.

- New Testament Studies. I am Pastor David Hale. I've been teaching this course for a few years now. My office hours are Monday mornings and Wednesday afternoons. The rest of the week, outside of this lecture, I'm off campus. Tutorial assignments are available in the Humanities building, near reception after this lecture. My office is in the same building but it's a bit of a rabbit warren to get there, so just ask reception, they'll point you in the right direction.

He could almost hear the slow blinks in the room.

- Your main assignment for the semester is an exegesis due in week 10. You'll be assigned the passages for that in your tutorials in week 3. There is an exam but it isn't too hard, so no need to worry about that just yet.

A student shuffled in their seat.

- You'll need to do all readings set. They are critical to keeping up with the tutorials and being able to do a good job on the exegesis. Some of the readings will push you. Maybe challenge you. That's a good thing. I want you to engage with that.

His ears popped.

- I want to make sure up front that we are all on the same page when it comes to this unit. This is theology, it is not Bible Studies. You do not, do not, need to be a believer to take this unit. This is not Bible College. It is not a seminary. We are engaging in critical study of the Bible as a text. Some of you may be studying to preach, that is fine. But some of you may be studying so you can become social workers, or because you find the topic interesting, perhaps you have a personal connection to the Church and you want to examine that in a deeper, more critical way. Regardless, belief is not a prerequisite and if you do believe, and that is not a bad thing, then I would ask that you don't ignore that in your studies but that you don't let it blind you when you approach your work. In your assignment, I will be expecting exegesis, not eisegesis.

Some students looked confused. There. He saw the students who were the true believers. A flash of consternation flitted across their faces. He would make sure they weren't in the same tutorial together.

- So what do we mean when we say exegesis? The literal meaning is to draw out. To bring the meaning of the text forth. What is the historical context of the text? Who was the author writing to and for? What was happening at that time that informs our understanding of the text. This is where we need to forego belief to properly grapple with the text. If you believe that the Bible is the divinely inspired word of God then you will struggle to be able to explore the text through that lens.

- Let's look at the Olivet Discourse, or Little Apocalypse, in Matthew 24 to 25, Mark 13 and Luke 21. How can we examine these texts in the gospel through exegesis? And why doesn't John share this same sermon? Well first, we need to look at when we believe the gospels were written.

He shuffled out into the cold evening air. The glow of the street lamps stretched out before him down the university street, the warm light catching the icy air. He pulled the collar of his jacket up.

He should go home. Anna would be getting home. Lisa would surely be around at some friend's house still. Probably Rachel. He didn't like Rachel much. She was too forthright in his presence. Too loud in a way that it seemed like Lisa was entertained by. Her parents didn't do much for him either. Perhaps he didn't like 16 year olds.

His ears popped.

He missed Lisa when she was 8. That was a good age. Clever. Delightful. Great company. Not so old that she thought she knew the world. Not so old that he didn't need him. Not so old that she wouldn't hold his hand.

Coming out of the university grounds, there was a bar across the road. It was warm there and they didn't care who you were. He stepped inside before he actively made the decision.

The bartender's beard was growing unruly. The bar hired students from the university to tend bar on the weekends when other students went. During the week it was locals and a local bartender. He put a beer down before David had even completed sitting down.

The bar mostly stocked cheap, harsh beer. The sort that had ether mixed in in years gone by.

The clientele down the bar were mixing politics in their cups. The university was progressive in the way that most universities were but dialled down in these later years of the century, long after the rage was no longer heavy in the air.

Once you stepped outside the grounds, the politics got mixed. The bar flys argued over global warming.

- Father, tell Trout here that he's wrong.

They knew him in this place.

- I'm not a priest, Jim. I'm a pastor. You and Trout have been arguing this for the last 6 months. I'm not wading in.

Jim grumbled.

Trout grumbled.

Misty put an oldie but a goodie on the jukebox.

- I've told you before Misty that we're not doing that.

The bartender didn't like it when you changed the atmosphere. Didn't mind it when the kids did it on the weekend but during the week this was his kingdom.

Misty was a lush and she'd be here until closing time. So would Jim and Trout. You'd get tourists stumble in every now and then but most would take a look through the window and know better.

David drained the beer and made a beeline for his coat. Anna would be waiting and Lisa still wouldn't be home. He shuffled towards home.

Anna was waiting with dinner when he got home. Some frozen thing that heated okay in the oven. He was sure it had a name on the box it came from but it came out tasting of mystery.

Anna sighed. She poured them glasses of red wine and went back to flicking through a book as she sat at the table.

- Don't forget I'm out tomorrow.

- Oh, yes, that had slipped my mind. What is it again?

- That show at the gallery. The one that Kim is putting on.

- Ah. The stages of Christ as... what was it... a dwarf of colour? Something like that.

Anna laughed softly and without feeling.

- No but sure. That. We're expecting protesters from the First Light Church.

- Idiots one and all.

- But they sure make a living

- Where's Lisa? She coming home tonight?

- Rachel's I assume.

- I mean...

- I know. I know. Linda is okay though. I'm not a fan of Stuart but...

- Yeah.

David moved into the living room and turned on the television.

- You going to come in when you're done?

- I might just head up. I'll need to get an early start. Alvin thinks he might have stumbled across something... I don't know. He said it could be revolutionary but you know how Al gets sometimes. Let's say it could be interesting.

- Okay but *Pummelled by Monkeys!* is on.

David liked *Pummelled by Monkeys!* Shrieks filled the air. He laughed. He was never sure why anyone would go on the show. But they always did.

He fell asleep, the sound of great apes hooting filling the air of the room.

———

COLD SUNLIGHT FILTERED into the room. Anna lightly stirred as David rose.

- I'm going to go for a run. I'll meet you up at the church later.

Anna groaned and turned to face his back.

- I've got some work I need to get done. We've got MVP due at the end of next week, so we're in crunch. I'll see you when you get home after.

Her voice sounded harsh. The scent of drink and smokes on her breath.

David leaned over and meant to kiss her cheek but missed and it landed on her ear.

- Love you.

- Love you.

The morning air was brittle. His lungs gasped as he ran down the street towards the church.

The church sat on a small hill, looking out over the old town. It had been a perfect location in years past. A central point that community could be grown around. A place where all were welcome and where the town came together.

Pushing open the weathered door, the place felt heavy with

the weight of that history. He'd let some kids film a horror movie in the building a couple of summers back.

There was a charm to the faded panelling and the slightly warped pews.

He went down to the basement. Showered and changed.

"Today, I want to talk about the wilderness. The wilderness that, I think, all of us know in some way. That place where certainty fades, where direction is lost, and we find ourselves... wandering.

"The Bible tells us that Christ himself spent forty days in the wilderness, tempted and tried. And we read that story and think, 'Well, of course he would survive. He's the Son of God. He has faith, unshakeable and eternal.' But when we imagine ourselves in that wilderness, stripped of all comforts, surrounded by silence... maybe it doesn't feel quite as simple.

"There's a certain kind of quiet out there, one that feels less like peace and more like absence. Some of us might even say it feels like... abandonment. That's a hard word, I know. But I think we need to speak honestly if we're to truly understand what it means to live a life of faith.

"I'm reminded of Psalm 22, where the psalmist cries out, 'My God, my God, why have you forsaken me?' It's raw, painful, and... vulnerable. Here we have a man who feels abandoned, left alone in his suffering. He is in the wilderness, pleading, but there's no answer, no comfort. Just... silence.

"Maybe you've felt that silence before. Maybe you've reached out in your own life—in moments of grief, or fear, or uncertainty—and heard nothing in return. Maybe you've found yourself wondering if there's anyone up there listening at all.

"In those moments, it can feel like faith is an illusion, like we're holding onto something that's slipping through our fingers. We come here each week, we sing the hymns, we pray, we tell each other that God is with us. But when we're alone, when we're lying awake in the dead of night... it's easy to wonder.

"But here's the thing about the wilderness: it strips away every-thing that isn't real. In the wilderness, there's no comfort, no safety net. There's just you, standing alone, with nothing but your doubts and fears. And maybe that's where real faith begins.

"Real faith isn't found in the easy answers or the comforting words. It isn't about feeling secure or finding assurance in every moment. Real faith is found in that place of doubt, in the struggle, in the silence. It's about standing in the wilderness, looking into the vast emptiness, and choosing—choosing to keep going.

"I wish I could stand here and tell you that faith always feels like a warm embrace, that it always gives us answers, that it always fills us with strength and certainty. But that isn't the reality of faith. At least, it isn't mine.

"Faith, for many of us, is more like a seed planted in barren ground. It takes time, it takes patience, and sometimes it takes more than we think we have to give. But if we're willing to let that seed grow in the silence, in the doubt, then maybe—just maybe—it'll take root. Maybe, one day, it will bloom.

"So if you find yourself in the wilderness today, if you feel that silence pressing in, remember that you're not alone. All of us, in some way, are walking through that wilderness. And maybe, just maybe, that's enough. Maybe all we need to know is that we're walking, that we haven't stopped, and that we're trying, each in our own way, to find our way back home.

"May we be brave enough to carry that silence. May we trust that, even if we can't feel it, even if we can't see it, there is some-thing… someone… guiding us through the wilderness. Amen."

He looked at his hand written notes he'd scrawled all over the page during the week. He couldn't give this sermon. Even if he felt every word of it in a place he couldn't quite pinpoint, Mrs. Peters wouldn't stand for it.

His ears popped.

Mrs. Peters would be here soon, no doubt, Ready to natter

at him about the readings and how she really likes that one hymn they used to sing when she was a child but wasn't such a fan of the hymns he chose. She had been close to his father. A real Christian's Christian. It was small wonder she hadn't made her way to First Light with the rest of them.

- Pastor Hale.

Her voice cut through him like ice. He braced himself and then came out of the basement with a broad smile he'd practised many times.

He moved to the pulpit and took a breath.

"I'd like us to think on a familiar story: the time Jesus spent in the wilderness. For forty days, he was alone, without comfort, tested and tempted, yet unwavering in his faith. It's a story that has always reminded me of the strength we're all asked to find within ourselves.

"The wilderness, as many of us know, is a place of challenge. It's that part of our lives where things seem uncertain, where we don't have the easy answers, where maybe we feel a bit... lost. We each have our own wilderness. It could be a difficult season of life, a moment of doubt, or a time when the answers we once found comfort in feel far away.

"When I think of Jesus in the wilderness, what strikes me is not just his endurance but his complete trust. He knew that even in isolation, even in hardship, God was with him. He didn't need reassurance at every step; his faith carried him. His example reminds us that faith isn't about having constant certainty or the answers laid out before us. Faith is about carrying on, even when the path is unclear.

"The psalmist writes, 'Even though I walk through the valley of the shadow of death, I will fear no evil, for you are with me.' There is a quiet strength in these words. They remind us that faith doesn't remove the shadows or the valleys from our lives. It doesn't promise us a life without struggle. What it does promise is that we are not alone in those moments. That even when we don't have the answers, we are held by something greater.

"I know that some of us here may feel like we're in our own wilderness right now. Life brings its share of trials, and it can feel, at times, like we're wandering without direction. But remember, just as Christ walked through his own wilderness, so too does our journey have purpose. It's in those very moments—when we feel stretched, when we feel uncertain—that our faith is being strengthened. It's through those trials that we find ourselves growing closer to God.

"We may not always understand the reasons for our struggles, and we may not always see where the path leads. But we can take comfort in knowing that our Lord has walked this path before us. We can draw strength from his example, trusting that God's hand guides us, even when the way isn't clear.

"Faith in the wilderness means trusting that God's purpose is at work, even when we cannot see it. It means believing that every step we take, no matter how difficult, brings us closer to Him. So today, if you find yourself facing a wilderness in your life, I encourage you to look to Christ's example. Walk forward with patience, with trust, and with faith that you are not alone.

"May we find strength in the journey, and may our faith carry us, even through the wilderness. Amen."

He sighed. He hadn't given too much of himself.

He looked out at his congregation, such as it was these days. Mrs. Peters in the front row. Old Timothy Runnels towards the back. He came some times but less so now his wife had passed. There was Paul Howard and Mark Hardy and Mrs. Walton. The totality of his flock. He was supposed to be getting a trainee in a few months.

There was another face out there that wasn't usually there. It looked like one of the students in the lecture hall the other day. One of the students that had looked less than pleased when he went on his discussion about not needing to believe to take the unit. His name was... David wasn't sure. John, he thought it could be.

As Mrs. Peters raised and started to lead the congregation in an impression of a rousing hymn, he turned his mind to how light the collection would be. Mrs. Peters would continue to tend to the garden as a gift to the church. His student left while Mrs. Peter was letting loose with her throaty warble.

The other congregants shuffled past, eyes down, mumbling thanks as he stood at the front door. Mrs. Peters spoke non stop at him.

- And it was a wonderful sermon today, Pastor Hale. We all struggle sometimes don't we. I know that Old Tim has seen his struggles. I worry about him now that Mrs. Runnels is gone. But what you said about trusting God's purpose, oh it just was exactly what I needed to hear today. Did I tell you I went to First Light with my daughter in law the other week? Oh, it was dreadful. It was so loud. And the fear they made me feel. Everything is the end. But I don't think that's what God's love is. God isn't to be feared. He is to be rejoiced. He is come. That's why I love your sermons. You may not have the certain something that your father had but I know that when I leave here every week, I feel nice. Very nice. I should make a meal for Old Tim. Oh my, did you see that Mr. Hardy was here today. I do need to catch up with him some time. Oh and that part that you said about...

Anna was hunched over her computer when he got home.

- Mrs. Peters says hi.

- And how is she these days? Won't stop talking?

- That's about right. I wonder if I could get some of the students to do some gardening. Something that would serve a purpose and get Mrs. Peters out of the way.

- Oh, you'd never. I can't imagine you'd try and do something that would put Mrs. Peters out. Lisa is out by the way.

- Do you want to...

- Crunch, remember.

- Sure, sure. But this week it'll be done yeah?

- Well, we'll get MVP done. Then who knows. I expect that the bosses will want some iterations on it. The hope is that we'll be able to package it by the end of the quarter.

- Still looking at the markets?

- That's part of it. I think that the bosses want it to be a bit more than that. They've been talking about it cutting across multiple items so it can capture more of a general business space than just the markets. Alvin has some stuff that he's pulling together that could extend it beyond even that.

David listened but not with intent.

- Can we try and make sure that Lisa is home for dinner this evening?

David's ears popped.

David sat in his office. The lights were dimmer than he wanted and than he'd imagined when they offered him a post at the university.

He wrestled with John 1:48 and the fig tree. The image called back to a metaphor for Israel in the Old Testament but was somewhat unique in the gospels. The cursing of the fig tree did not appear in John, so the imagery served a different purpose. Or was a shorthand in speaking to the Johannite community.

A quiet knock came at the door. Standing there was the student from the service on Sunday. His smile did little to mask the cold look in his eyes.

- David? Do you mind if I call you David, sir?

- That's fine. It was John wasn't it?

- That's right, sir, John Michaels. I'm in your New Testament Studies class.

- That's right, I remember you. You came on Sunday, didn't

you?'There certainly isn't an expectation that students attend my sermons.

- Well, that is what I wanted to talk to you about. Do you have time at the moment?

- Of course, come in. I'm always available during office hours.

- Thank you, that's very kind of you. The other day in class you talked about belief.

- Yes. It's something I start that particular class with every year. I think it's good to be inclusive and also to set the tone.

- I think it's unacceptable.

- I'm sorry that you feel that way, John. However, that is the nature of the class and how I teach it and I'm unlikely to change that.

- I think you should reconsider.

- I always welcome the feedback of my students and ways they think that I could improve the class but this is one area I'm probably not going to change.

- I'll be making a complaint to the head of school. I think that it's terrible. I went to your sermon on Sunday so I could make sure I wasn't wrong. You aren't a Christian and yet you think you have any right to teach the word of the Lord. I told Pastor Doug at First Light…

- Ah, Doug. How is Doug these days?

- He is a real, true believer. He knows the Lord.

- Please calm down, John.

- Pastor Doug told me you'd always been like this and your father before you.

- Please calm down, or I will ask you to leave, John.

- I will be putting in a formal complaint.

- And I welcome reading it, now if you'll please leave my office.

David was laid out on the couch. His head hurt. One too many wines.

Anna stood in the door of the room watching the television. The news was the normal run down of stabbings, shootings and odd local stories.

- Just waiting for the business update and then I'll head to bed. You think you'll be long?

- I want to wait up for Lisa to get in. I think we need to talk to her.

- She's 16, D. What are we going to say that's going to have an effect?

- We should try.

- Maybe but maybe we should just let her be. A couple of years from now and she'll be heading towards college and then she'll be gone. I don't know... I miss her.

- I get that.

- You remember how she used to be when she was a kid? When we'd read her those books... you remember those? That series about that kid girl detective?

- Sure. Ellie Sleuth Adventures.

- You remember that really dumb one about the sneakers that went missing.

- Sure.

- I miss that kid.

- And I get that but she was never going to be that kid forever.

- I know. I know. I just.

The business update was on, so Anna stopped paying attention to him.

- Alvin's new model predicted that.

David's ears popped.

- I'm heading to bed. Come up soon. If she gets in before you get to bed, great. If not, she's a good kid. She'll be fine.

THE COLOSSAL Humanoid in the Stratosphere: What We Know So Far

In an event that continues to defy all comprehension, a massive humanoid figure has appeared within Earth's stratosphere, just beneath the edge of space. This towering figure, resembling a human body but on an unimaginable scale, stretches across vast swaths of the sky. Its presence is so enormous and unyielding that it casts a significant shadow over the landscape below.

Here's what we know so far.

What exactly is the object?

The object is a colossal, human-like figure positioned in the stratosphere, approximately 30-50 kilometres above Earth's surface. It appears to be in a stable orbit over Spain. Estimates place the figure at around 160 kilometres in height, dwarfing anything seen before in human history. Its shape mirrors that of a human body, complete with arms, legs, a torso, and a head, making it eerily familiar yet utterly alien.

Though its surface appears to be organic, no one has been able to determine exactly what material it is composed of. It is solid, casting a vast shadow across the ground, and its dimensions are stable. Despite initial fears, the figure has not moved or shown indication that it will move or take any action.. The figure appears inert, though the humanoid form has led to considerable speculation about its nature and purpose.

How did it get there?

The most perplexing aspect of the figure's appearance is how it came to occupy the stratosphere. Unlike objects placed in space by human activity, there was no indication of its arrival, no warning of a massive incoming body. Its presence was first observed simultaneously from multiple regions across Europe, suggesting that it materialised suddenly.

Satellite imagery shows no signs of propulsion or transport mechanisms, and no atmospheric disturbances were recorded that could explain such a massive structure being placed into the stratosphere. One prevailing theory is that it appeared instantaneously, but how—or by whom—remains an open question. Some experts suggest that it may have been cloaked or hidden in some way, only becoming visible once it settled into its current position. How this would have been achieved is unclear as no government on earth currently has acquired such technology on a scale that would support this.

Is it an alien life form?

The humanoid appearance has led to rampant speculation about extraterrestrial involvement. Its form, proportionally similar to a human, seems unlikely to be a natural phenomenon. However, there is no evidence that the figure is alive—it has not moved or demonstrated any biological processes.

Nevertheless, the fact that it so closely resembles a human body raises questions about its origin. Is this the work of an advanced civilization, or is it some form of signal or monument? There's no consensus, and researchers caution against jumping to conclusions. For now, the figure is being treated as a non-living object, but scientists are open to any new data that could emerge.

Is it dangerous?

We don't know. At present, there is no direct evidence to suggest that the figure poses an immediate threat to Earth. However, its mere presence is causing significant concern. Being situated in the stratosphere means that it occupies a part of the atmosphere where Earth's weather systems form.

The figure's vast shadow is expected to have an observable

impact on the regions beneath it, cooling the climate locally and altering weather patterns. Scientists are also concerned about long-term atmospheric effects. The fact that the body is stationary in the sky means it's creating permanent disruptions in air circulation and potentially affecting global weather systems.

There's also the looming question: what happens if it moves? Given its immense size, even the slightest shift could lead to catastrophic damage on the ground.

How are world governments responding?

The appearance of the figure has thrown world governments into a state of disarray. Emergency summits have been convened by the United Nations, while individual nations have scrambled to assess the potential threat. Some countries have declared states of emergency, while Spain has issued evacuation orders for areas directly under the figure's shadow, fearing potential fallout from its unknown impact on the atmosphere.

There is talk of an international mission to study the figure up close, but the logistics of such an operation are staggering. With the object being located so high in the atmosphere, it poses significant challenges for both manned and unmanned missions. Nevertheless, pressure is mounting for a global response.

What are the scientific implications?

The figure has created a seismic shift in the scientific community. Its existence challenges everything we know about physics, biology, and space. If it is a natural phenomenon, scientists are struggling to explain how something of this scale and precision could form. If it is artificial, the questions multiply exponentially: Who created it? Why? And how did they manage to place it within Earth's atmosphere?

Simply the fact that it appears to be maintaining a geosynchronous orbit in the stratosphere, which should not be physically possible, has the scientific community wondering if much of what they assumed about the workings of the planet, and potentially the universe, were simply wrong.

Researchers are using every available tool—satellites, drones, and ground-based observatories—to gather data on the figure. However, the stratosphere is a challenging environment to study, and the sheer size of the object is complicating efforts to fully understand its nature. A number of researchers have wondered whether this will ultimately be a momentary anomaly. Though others question whether that would lead to even more queries and theorising than if the figure becomes a more permanent feature.

What's next?

As the world struggles to adjust to the sight of the enormous figure in the sky, many are left with more questions than answers. Perhaps most importantly, what does it mean for humanity?

For now, the figure remains silent and still, a looming presence that casts both literal and figurative shadows over the Earth. Whether it is a harbinger of something greater or merely a passive anomaly, it has already irrevocably changed the way we see our place in the universe.

What we don't know

What it is.

Where it came from.

What it may do.

THE WARMTH of the bar fed into his bones. The shag carpet crunching under his shoes from decades of nights gone on too long and too recklessly.

- I don't know, Jim. I don't know, Trout.

- But someone there at the university must have some ideas?

Jim nodded as he spoke, his head growing heavy from an afternoon of drink.

- There's not much of that. There's a few professors that do some research stuff but we aren't really a place that survives on that sort of thing. We aren't pulling much in the way of grants for sciences.

- But there's a whole bunch of people like you, Father. Smart people that have studied.

- I'm not a Catholic, Jim.

Misty sauntered over to the bar. The bartender put another glass of wine in front of her and plopped down another beer in front of David. The television, high in the corner, showed The Body. That's what television was now. The past week and a half, it was only The Body and if the stations tried to show anything else, people would just change to channels that showed The Body.

Misty leaned in close, in the way she often would when David was in the bar.

- It's the return. He's back, Pastor.

- It's an alien mega structure is what it is. Something that high up, just lying there. There's no way it could do that if it wasn't from something out there.

Trout was propping his head up on a fist.

- No. No! Trout, I keep telling you. It's not anything like that. It's not there at all. It's a hologram. They can do that. Look there.

The bartender pointed at the television. They all turned and stared at it for a silent moment.

- There. That. You see that? That little flicker just then. It's a hologram.

- Your TV is garbage, Rick. That's what that is. You think that everyone would stop what they were doing and the world would stop and we'd all just be staring at it for days and it's just make believe?

- What's the hologram for?

- Viral marketing. I don't know what it is yet but you watch, this'll all be to get us to buy something.

- It's God. Tell them, Pastor.

- I don't know what it is. None of us do. Maybe it's God. Maybe it's a hologram. Maybe it's the solution to food security and we won't need to go to the store anymore cause whatever that thing is will feed us for the rest of our lives. Maybe it's some poor sap that got caught up in... something and now he's a giant floating in the sky and he's terrified and maybe he'll fall from the sky.

- Ah well, would just be the Spanish that take the brunt of that.

- I don't know. You don't know. Let me drink.

They turned back to the television and watched.

Around Alvin's desk, Anna could see about half of the development team. Alvin sat in the middle, close to his monitor. The team looked excited, chattering the way they did when someone stumbled across a solve that had taken weeks.

The MVP had been pushed out. The bosses seemed pleased and had given the go ahead for the package to go into production. The sales guys had been ready to go before The Body appeared. Now there was uncertainty and whispers that cutbacks were coming. She wasn't sure whether to stick close to Alvin or be far enough away that when the cuts came down she'd be overlooked.

She wandered over to see what the commotion was. She wanted to get out and get home. David wasn't doing much of anything at the moment, he wasn't really there but that was hardly a change. She wanted to be home for Lisa. Lisa. She didn't know what she was going to do there.

- What's going on?

The team turned to face her. Alvin stayed hunched over the keyboard. At the other end of the floor she could see non stop coverage of The Body on a TV.

Sarah responded in a hush.

- It's Al's new model.

- Al, we've talked about this.

Alvin still didn't turn as he spoke.

- This is different, Anna. This is something else.

- MVP is done, we just need to pull together the package now.

James flashed her a look of annoyance.

- And the point of the package now is what? Everything is out the window. You know there's cuts coming, we all do. So why do the package. The markets have dived. The only news now is that thing up there. You want to waste time on the package, go for it.

- Piss off, James. Then why do a new model, Alvin? The fundamentals are completely gone, there's no way to calibrate for what is happening now and what might come next. It's not your model's fault it didn't see this coming.

Some smirks from the team. Alvin snorted.

- Anna, grab your machine. We'll jump in one of the rooms.

- Can we tomorrow? I want to get out. I'm exhausted. Aren't you exhausted? I was running on fumes for crunch and now I want to get out on time.

- We can. But you want to see this.

- Fine. Fine. Five minutes tops.

Alvin shuffled into the room. He looked tired. His facial hair was getting out of hand. She worried about him sometimes.

- I worry about you sometimes.

- No need. Now. What are our constraints?

- Oh, god. I didn't come in here for something we both know. Dataset size. Compute. I guess, energy?

- Exactly. Compute we can deal with, we've got a team and the hardware that can keep up most of the time. Energy, whatever. I'm not paying the bills, you aren't paying the bills. But data, that's the thing.

- And always will be. That's why we build models. What's the smallest size that we need to get to a solid predictor. That's the game.

- What if it wasn't?

- As in you had as much data as you could consume?

- Yes.

- Well, sure, that would be great. Would allow us to calibrate further, would mean we can dial in results during training. That's why we chose the markets in the first place for the model. That and there's a customer base for it. It's why those poll aggregator hacks get it wrong all the time.

- Yes. Yes. The markets. But what if it could be more than that?

- Like building in something like trade flows? Like a value add for the model? I don't know what we're talking about here. I'm tired. I want to get out of here, Al.

- What if I told you the model did predict The Body?

- Sorry. It didn't. No one could have seen something like that happen. Or do you mean that the model showed a probability of the markets crashing? The model always has some outliers on every run like that. There's always a chance tomorrow is Black Monday. So you saw a crash in the outputs and you think the model predicted a gigantic body appearing in the sky? Al, you need rest.

- No, not that model. That thing is child's play. Good

enough for the bosses, gets the job done. Not good enough for you and me.

Anna shifted. The chairs in these rooms had never been good. One of the many ways they kept people from long meetings.

Alvin moved over to the screen on the wall and plugged his laptop into it.

- If we're not talking about that model then what am I doing here, Al? Just let me get out of here and whatever this is you can show me tomorrow morning. I've got a meeting first thing and then I'm all yours and we can do this but my head is pounding.

On the screen, Alvin brought up a terminal window.

- I thought we agreed on the UI for this, don't tell me you got the team to play with it again and we need to be dealing with the command line again. We put that to bed when we hit MVP.

- I'm telling you, not that model. This is Pythia. This is something else entirely.

- Al, what the hell? A new model. Is this going to be the next revision? We aren't anywhere near that yet. We need to see how everything shakes out and if we even get to the package at this point.

- Datasets are our constraint. What if you could consume considerably more data across everything?

- Everything? Like cross industry? Multiple sectors?

- Stop thinking of the markets. Pythia isn't for that. This isn't about the markets. It's not about business. This is more than that.

- So other disciplines? Like you've made a model that predicts the markets and baseball?

- Yes, baseball. Good. That and everything. But down to a

level we haven't been able to go before. Not just baseball but baseball players.

- Well, most models would adjust for age, playstyle, past performance.

- Not that. At the individual level. Like each player. Not just this player is a certain sort of player but this player is this individual player who has wants and needs and grew up somewhere and will age and die and maybe they make it to 100 or they could die at 40 from a heart attack that no one saw coming.

- Al, you need time off. Crunch has done something to you. You know how you sound right? That's not possible.

Did he know how he sounded?

- It wasn't possible but Pythia can go to that level. The problem we run into is people. Underlying all that data we feed into a model is people. We can classify and trend and predict on that but people. They aren't rational. We assume that if we classify people into groups then those groups will act in a certain way which will mean that something like a stock will go one way or the other. But they don't, Anna, they don't. They do weird things like buy things that are bad for them, or they take out a loan that they can't afford. They don't optimise, they aren't efficient.

- Sure. I mean, prediction is always fuzzy. I mean, if it was perfect then there'd be no need to run the outputs as many times as we do. What's the most probable outcome given the data? But even if you could get perfect data, and you can't, you'd still just be looking at probabilities.

- Pythia predicted The Body.

- Sorry, what?

- Pythia. She predicted The Body.

- You've lost me. As in I'm going home.

Anna stood to leave the room.

- Please wait, just a minute or two more.

- I think you need to talk to someone, Al.

- I want to talk to you about this. The team is all a chattering mass as they always get but I want you to see this. I want you to be part of this, Anna.

- But you're telling me that this model…

- Pythia.

- This model Pythia. It predicted The Body. It predicted something appearing in the sky out of nowhere that no one can explain. That looks like maybe it breaks physics. It predicted that?

- Okay, maybe not exactly The Body. But it's like it predicted the space The Body would take up. It wasn't high probability but out of nowhere it was throwing up runs that had Spain in darkness, shifts in the climate in Europe, significant ones not just normal trend but that some external factor was entering the system to cause those effects.

- How? That isn't possible.

- I've put pretty much everything in there. That's what I'm trying to tell you. It has consumed, and is still consuming, so much that we can use it for anything. It's gaming out the whole world with precision.

Anna felt the hairs on her arm raise.

- Al. How are you doing this?

- I don't want to get into the datasets. I know you wouldn't approve. Let's just say there's some stuff in there that I maybe shouldn't have. Plus vision sets, there's quite a bit that's pulling from sat constellations to bump up the raw data. It's a lot. It's near enough to everything that I could get.

- And then what?

- It's deep machine learning. It's pretty cool stuff but it's the dataset that makes it possible.

- I don't know, Al. Have you been using the servers here for compute?

Alvin didn't reply.

- Al. Come on. You know there is talk of cutbacks. You can't be doing this, you'll end up getting cut if they find out.

- I know. I know, okay. But there's nowhere else I can get access to. I mean, maybe you could talk to David or something and see if he can get me an in at the university and I could piggyback on their hardware.

- No. Plus, you know that place won't have what you need for this.

- You sound like you want in

Anna didn't reply.

Cold night air brushing her face. Lisa ran, her legs pumping under her. Brody whooped. Lisa whooped. Rachel whooped. She closed her eyes and ran. In the stands she could hear Megan. Sweet Megan. She ran back towards the stands so she could watch Brody and Rachel. They'd fallen into a heap on the field. Their limbs tangled together. Megan passed her the bottle and she drank, the amber liquid burning on the way down. She looked at Megan and smiled. Megan smiled back, a twinkle hiding there. She brushed her hair. Megan said that she thought they should head to the woods. There were things in the woods. Rachel and Brody were pulling each other's clothes off. She stood and shouted into the night. The sound carried up into the sky.

WE FIND ourselves living in extraordinary times. Something we have no precedent for. This enormous figure, hanging above us in the sky, silent and still. People are afraid. People are confused. Many are searching for answers, and many more are questioning where God is in all of this.

I want to start today by acknowledging those fears and doubts. It's natural to feel uncertain when the world shifts in ways we can't comprehend. But I want to remind you all that we've been here before—not with this exact event, of course, but with the feeling of facing the unknown, of grappling with forces beyond our control.

In the face of uncertainty, it is easy to be consumed by fear. Some look to the skies now and see a looming threat, an omen of doom. Others feel abandoned, as though this strange phenomenon means that God has left us, has taken his leave of us. God is not absent. God is with us, even now, even in this.

Psalm 46 reminds us that God is "our refuge and strength, an ever-present help in trouble." These words were written in a time when the people of Israel faced chaos and destruction, when it felt like the very ground beneath them might fall away. It was a time of victory, but a time of uncertainty. But the psalmist tells them—and tells us—not to fear, even if the mountains collapse and the seas rise up. And let's be honest: seeing a figure hanging in the sky as large as a city—well, that can certainly make us feel like the mountains are falling.

But what does the psalm tell us to do? It doesn't ask us to ignore our fear, but to bring it before God. It asks us to place our trust in God's refuge, in God's unwavering strength. This figure, whatever it is, does not change who God is. It doesn't shake God's foundation. It doesn't alter the fact that God is still present, still active, still loving us as we try to make sense of this new reality.

I know some of you are asking, "What is this thing? Why is it here?" And the truth is, I don't know. I don't know. None of us know. I'm not a physicist or any other type of scientist that could have an idea of what this is or what it means. The scientists are puzzled. And in times like this, where our knowledge falls short, it's tempting to either fall into speculation or retreat into fear. I've heard the rumors, the theories—everything from aliens to divine messengers to apocalyptic signs.

But we must be careful. We are called to live by faith

David caught himself for a moment.

Not by fear or speculation. When we let fear drive us, we lose sight of the One who holds all things together. We risk losing sight of the God who has walked with humanity through every unknown, through every storm, through every upheaval in history.

Faith is not the absence of questions; it's not the absence of doubt. Faith is trusting in God even when the answers don't come easily, even when we face mysteries that defy explanation. Faith is believing that, even when something incomprehensible hangs above us, God's love remains steadfast.

I don't know.

I don't know.

I just.

David stopped. He looked out at the congregation. There was Mrs. Peters, waiting for the next words. The pews had thinned more than normal. He caught his voice and continued.

We must hold fast to our hope. Romans 5:5 tells us that "hope does not disappoint us, because God's love has been poured into our hearts through the Holy Spirit." Hope is not wishful thinking; it's the assurance that God is at work, even when we can't see the full picture. It's the belief that, whatever this figure may mean, God's purposes for humanity are good and loving.

Second, we must respond with love. That is what Christ taught us, again and again. This is a time of chaos. I don't know what comes next. I don't know what this means. We need to...

What? He was hardly the one to be providing people with guidance.

There is a shadow of something that we do not understand. I don't have the answers. Maybe God does. I hope that we can come together during this time and just be there for each other.

Amen.

USER: SKYWATCHER666
DATE: OCTOBER 12, 20XX
WHAT IS REALLY GOING ON WITH THAT MASSIVE HUMANOID FIGURE IN THE SKY?? THE NEWS IS ACTING LIKE THEY DON'T HAVE ANY ANSWERS, BUT COME ON, HOW COULD SOMETHING THAT BIG JUST APPEAR OUT OF NOWHERE AND NOBODY SAW IT COMING?? I'M TELLING YOU RIGHT NOW, THERE'S MORE TO THIS THAN THEY'RE LETTING ON. I'VE BEEN DIGGING INTO THIS, AND I DON'T THINK THIS IS JUST SOME RANDOM SPACE OBJECT. THIS IS DELIBERATE.

USER: TRUTHSEEKER77
YOU'RE NOT WRONG, MAN. COVER-UP. HOW DOES SOMETHING THE SIZE OF A CITY JUST APPEAR IN GEOSYNCHRONOUS ORBIT? NO WARNING, NO DETECTION FROM NASA, ESA, ANYONE? OUR SPACE AGENCIES SPEND THE MONEY OF A SMALL COUNTRY MONITORING THE SKIES, BUT THEY'RE "SURPRISED" BY THIS? NOT BUYING IT.
I'VE BEEN HEARING WHISPERS THAT THIS THING MIGHT HAVE BEEN CLOAKED—MAYBE FOR YEARS. THERE'S NO WAY IT JUST SHOWED UP WITHOUT SOME ADVANCED TECH KEEPING IT HIDDEN. ALIEN TECH? SECRET GOVERNMENT PROJECT? EITHER WAY, THEY KNOW WAY MORE THAN THEY'RE TELLING US.

USER: ALIENENIGMA
EXACTLY! AND LET'S NOT IGNORE THE SHAPE.
IT'S HUMANOID. NOT SOME ASTEROID OR SPACE
DEBRIS, BUT SOMETHING THAT LOOKS LIKE US.
THAT'S TOO SPECIFIC TO BE A COINCIDENCE.
MAYBE IT'S A WARNING, OR MAYBE IT'S BEEN
PUT THERE DELIBERATELY BY A MORE ADVANCED
SPECIES. HELL, WHAT IF IT'S BEEN WATCHING US
THIS WHOLE TIME?
AND WHY HASN'T THERE BEEN ANY MAJOR
GOVERNMENT RESPONSE? NO MASS
EVACUATIONS, NO MILITARY MOBILIZATION?
EITHER THEY KNOW IT'S NOT A THREAT BECAUSE
THEY'VE BEEN EXPECTING IT, OR THEY'RE HIDING
SOMETHING EVEN BIGGER. I WOULDN'T BE
SURPRISED IF THERE'S BEEN CONTACT ALREADY
AND THEY'RE KEEPING IT QUIET.

USER: REDPILLPHILOSOPHER
THINK ABOUT THIS FOR A SECOND: WHY DOES IT
LOOK HUMAN? IF IT'S ALIEN, WHY WOULD IT BE
SHAPED LIKE US? MY THEORY: WE'RE PART OF
SOME KIND OF EXPERIMENT. WHAT IF WE WERE
MADE BY THESE BEINGS, AND NOW THEY'RE
CHECKING IN ON US? THAT FIGURE COULD BE A
SYMBOL OR AN ENFORCER. MAYBE WE'VE HIT
SOME KIND OF MILESTONE, AND NOW THEY'RE
HERE TO REMIND US WHO'S REALLY IN CHARGE.
AND DON'T GET ME STARTED ON HOW THE
MAINSTREAM MEDIA IS BARELY COVERING THIS.
THEY WANT TO KEEP US CALM, KEEP US FROM
ASKING QUESTIONS. BUT WE SHOULD BE ASKING
THEM ALL THE QUESTIONS. WHY HASN'T ANY
FOOTAGE BEEN RELEASED FROM UP CLOSE?
WHERE ARE THE SATELLITE IMAGES? YOU'RE
TELLING ME THEY HAVEN'T SENT ANY DRONES
OR PROBES UP THERE YET? RIDICULOUS.

USER: THEREALINSIDER
YOU'RE ON THE RIGHT TRACK. I WORK IN
AEROSPACE, AND LET'S JUST SAY I'VE HEARD
THINGS. THERE'S DEFINITELY A MISSION BEING
PLANNED TO GET UP CLOSE, BUT THEY'RE
KEEPING IT UNDER WRAPS. THEY DON'T WANT A
GLOBAL PANIC. CAN YOU IMAGINE HOW PEOPLE
WOULD FREAK OUT. THE FIGURE ISN'T JUST
SITTING THERE; FROM WHAT I'VE HEARD, IT'S
EMITTING SOME KIND OF SIGNAL OR PULSE—
SOMETHING THAT'S AFFECTING OUR SATELLITES
AND COMMUNICATIONS. THIS THING DIDN'T JUST
APPEAR; IT WAS PLACED THERE DELIBERATELY,
PROBABLY A LONG TIME AGO, AND WE'VE ONLY
JUST NOW BEEN ALLOWED TO SEE IT.

USER: SERPENTSKEPTIC
DUDE, IF THAT'S TRUE, WE'RE IN WAY DEEPER
THAN WE THOUGHT. I'VE BEEN SAYING FOR
YEARS THAT GOVERNMENTS HAVE BEEN
WORKING WITH ENTITIES THAT AREN'T FROM
EARTH. THIS COULD BE A POWER MOVE, LIKE A
CHECKMATE. WE'VE ADVANCED TOO FAR, AND
NOW WE'RE BEING REMINDED THAT WE'RE NOT
AT THE TOP OF THE FOOD CHAIN. THE ELITES
DEFINITELY KNOW MORE THAN WE DO—THEY
ALWAYS DO. THEY'RE EITHER IN ON IT, OR
THEY'RE PREPARING THEIR ESCAPE ROUTES
WHILE THE REST OF US ARE LEFT TO DEAL WITH
WHATEVER THIS THING IS.

USER: EYESOPENWIDE
IT'S ALL STARTING TO MAKE SENSE NOW. HAVE
YOU NOTICED THE UPTICK IN "DISCLOSURE"
STORIES LATELY? GOVERNMENTS
DECLASSIFYING UAP FILES, MILITARY PILOTS
TALKING ABOUT "UNEXPLAINED PHENOMENA"—
IT'S ALL BEEN BUILDING TO THIS. THEY'VE BEEN
PREPPING US, CONDITIONING US TO ACCEPT
THAT SOMETHING BIGGER IS COMING.
NOW, THIS FIGURE SHOWS UP AND THEY'RE
ACTING LIKE IT'S NO BIG DEAL? PLEASE.
WHATEVER'S GOING ON UP THERE, THEY'VE
KNOWN ABOUT IT FOR A LONG TIME, AND THIS IS
JUST THE BEGINNING. I THINK WE'RE ABOUT TO
SEE THE NEXT PHASE OF THE "PLAN." I HOPE
EVERYONE'S READY.

USER: FINALAWAKENING
LOOK, THEY'RE NOT GOING TO TELL US THE
TRUTH. THE GOVERNMENTS, THE
CORPORATIONS, THE MILITARY—THEY'RE ALL IN
BED WITH EACH OTHER. WHATEVER THIS THING
IS, IT'S PART OF A BIGGER AGENDA. MAYBE IT'S
SURVEILLANCE, MAYBE IT'S A PRECURSOR TO
SOMETHING WORSE. BUT THE FACT IS, WE ARE
THE LAST TO KNOW. WE NEED TO STAY VIGILANT
AND QUESTION EVERYTHING. THE GIANT IN THE
SKY IS JUST THE START. WHAT'S COMING NEXT IS
WHAT WE SHOULD BE REALLY WORRIED ABOUT.

USER: SKYWATCHER666
COULDN'T AGREE MORE. I THINK WE'RE BEING
PREPPED FOR SOMETHING WAY BEYOND WHAT
WE CAN EVEN IMAGINE. THE FIGURE IN THE SKY
IS JUST A SIGN, BUT WE HAVE TO CONNECT THE
DOTS. STAY WOKE, EVERYONE, AND KEEP
DIGGING FOR THE TRUTH. THEY CAN'T KEEP THE
LID ON THIS FOREVER.

USER: OBSERVER420
GUYS, HAS ANYONE ELSE NOTICED WEIRD
WEATHER PATTERNS SINCE THIS THING SHOWED
UP? I'VE BEEN TRACKING SOME STRANGE
FLUCTUATIONS THAT STARTED RIGHT AFTER THE
FIGURE APPEARED. COINCIDENCE? I THINK NOT.
I'M TELLING YOU, THIS IS AFFECTING MORE
THAN JUST OUR SATELLITES. BRACE
YOURSELVES—THIS IS JUST THE TIP OF THE
ICEBERG.

DAVID SLOUCHED ON THE COUCH, the remote clutched loosely in one hand. He flicked through channels trying to find something to watch, trying to find something that would fill the hole in his head that wanted to be entertained. The screen flickered as he moved through the channels, nothing catching his attention. There was a pit in him. Colours flitting across his face. Static and grabs of sound filling the room. He felt hungry.

Click.

"…body spotted in the sky over Spain, raising questions about—"

Click.

"…NEW! Miracle Complexion Cream! Look younger, feel younger! Turn back the clock—"

Click.

A gameshow host shouts, "That's a WIN! You've got $10,000, and now…" a bloodied, almost human form staggering out of a caravan.

Click.

A low voice narrates over the image of a lion stalking across a dry savannah, "…each movement, a masterclass in the art of survival…"

Click.

"Scientists are scrambling for answers, but so far, nothing." A chyron reads: "Physicists puzzled.

Click.

"...and she didn't even tell him she was in love with his brother! *You have to tell him, Dana!*"

Click.

"...join the thousands who've already experienced the difference. Order today for only $29.99, and receive..."

Click.

"It's been days since the figure appeared, and governments worldwide are..."

Click.

"Just a touch of rosemary to bring out the flavour, and... oh, look at that! Perfection!"

Click.

"...our cameras captured these strange new patterns in animal migration, as if the entire ecosystem is shifting—"

Click.

"Buy one, get one free! Don't miss out on the deal of a lifetime—"

Click.

"We're witnessing the end times! Brothers and sisters, prepare your hearts, for the hour is near... pick up that phone now, our operators are waiting to talk your call so you can donate today..."

Click.

A sitcom laugh track rolls as a man stumbles over a chair. "I swear, honey, I'll fix it tomorrow!"

Click.

"...military forces have been placed on high alert as tensions continue to escalate. However, no word yet on a—"

Click.

A soft piano plays as a woman gazes out a rain-streaked window, whispering, "How do we go on? How do we live with the weight of…"

Click.

"…sleep is crucial for brain health, so don't skip out on a full night's…"

Click.

"The blue whale, the largest animal on Earth, drifts gracefully through its ocean kingdom, but predators lurk…"

Click.

"PUMMELLED BY MONKEYS! Brought to you by Elevate Impact Ventures…

Click.

"A joint European-American mission to study the figure is planned for the coming days. Reports are that Tuesday is expected to have favourable conditions. Trevor Mangian, billionaire philanthropist, is said to be…"

Click.

"…and the sale is only available this weekend! Don't miss out on our incredible discounts!"

Click.

"…impossible. We're talking about a phenomenon beyond anything we've ever—"

Click.

"Oh, come on, Steve! You can't honestly believe that thing's real!"

Click.

David stopped flashing through the stations and kept it on the news. The body loomed in the frame, haunting the television like it had come to haunt every day.

The news anchor looked tired. Days of trying to get the news out of no changes but everyone watching.

Anna stood in the doorway, the television lighting her in shadow.

- That cooking show looked okay, what were they making?

- Don't know, nothing is on.

- You need to stop looking at it. There's other things in the world, other things happening. I'm here.

- Is there? Seems like everywhere is all just about the body.

- How's work going?

- A kid is making a complaint about me. He knows Doug.

- Are you worried? Should I be worried?

- It's never anything more than just a kid doing the wrong course, or thinking they're doing the right course and I'm teaching it wrong. I should have taken that grant the other year.

- I know but it wasn't the right time. Lisa was just about to start high school, we couldn't just pick up and move to Greece cause you wanted to research sexuality in the ancient world.

- I know. I know. It made sense but I wasn't cut out for teaching.

- What do you want to do then? Do you want to leave the university? Maybe just preach?

- Good job I've done there too. Taken what my dad built and just had it wither. If you didn't have your job then I'm not sure...

- Is that what this is? You care that you aren't making money. Babe, if you wanted money then why did you ever follow your dad into the church? Not sure that's the ideal path to get to riches. I mean, if you want that then why don't you go and talk to Doug.

David couldn't respond to that.

- It's never been about that right? I mean, you care more about community and people like Mrs. Peters finding their way to God and all that, right?

- I...

- Well, what do you want to do? I can carry the load for a bit if you need to take time away from everything?

- I... I'm not sure. I don't know if it's that, I don't know if it's this thing up there, I don't... Look, it's late, I'm tired, let's not. How are things at work?

- I'm worried about Alvin.

- What's new.

- Nom he's talking about something that... he sounds like he's really starting to break. Maybe we pushed him too hard during crunch.

- Does anyone ever push Alvin to do anything he doesn't want?

- No. Sure. He says that he's built something that predicts everything.

- I don't know what that means.

- Not just the markets like we do, he is saying everything. The world type everything.

- That is also something that I don't understand.

- He thinks... he says... that he has built a model that can go down to an individual level so it can account for people doing the sort of things that people do.

- Right, got it, math stuff that I will never get.

- I mean, yes but there's no way that what he's talking about is possible. It's just... it's not... I'm worried about him.

Silence passed between them.

- I'm going to head up. I'll see you soon?

- Sure. Can we try and get all of us home for dinner at some point this week?

- You can call Lisa you know?

- I feel like we need to be together at the moment.

David went back to staring at the screen. The body looked

like it warped light around it when you stared at it too long. The figure filled the frame and then his eyes and then it felt like there was weight coming at him, pushing him further into the couch.

———

THE MAN STOPPED.

He would never be sure why he stopped at that moment right then.

Cold wind blew on his face.

The weather had set in in a way he didn't remember.

He stopped.

His feet felt as though they wouldn't move from the spot, like quicksand had formed on the snow dusted hill top.

In the days that would come, he would codify the feeling as being watched. He was watched.

He looked to the sky. Clear inky darkness. A light glow from the town below. Stars. The stars pushed down on him.

He couldn't see the figure. Not from here. He knew it was out there, far from his sight. He could feel the figure. The gigantic form made him feel heavier than he remembered.

As the chilled sun came up the next morning, the man still looked to the sky.

Later that morning, a man approached him. The man muttered a good morning as he passed the man looking at the sky.

The man continued to look at the sky, his eyes slowly blinking.

The other man stopped. He repeated his greeting. Nothing. No response.

The other man walked to him.

- Hello.

Nothing.

- Hello?

The man looked at the sky. He did not flinch.

- HELLO.

The man barely batted an eyelid as he gazed through the sky.

- What are you doing? Can you hear me?

The man did hear him but he was bound to the ground and would only watch the sky. He watched the sky as he was watched back.

Over the day more people walked past. More people would try and get his attention. Most wandered off after they failed to get his attention. Some would stop and see if they could see what he looked at. They could not see beyond the sparse clouds.

On the second day, more people walked past.

It was when multiple people tried to get his attention that a crowd began to form.

The crowd was angry at the lack of his response.

They demanded to know what he was looking at. And why he wouldn't move. And why he would not acknowledge them.

He continued to stare at the sky.

He blinked.

The crowd grew from three to five to ten, doubling as more people going about their day walked past and wondered why this crowd stood where they were.

The man turned to the crowd, breaking his eye contact with the sky, and looked at the people to his side.

- It is up there. We are being watched.

The crowd turned their faces to the sky and they remained.

VIDEO:

A bustling street in Barcelona. The point of view moves through a crowd of people. Bad audio comes through the cheap microphone on the phone. Traffic noises are too loud. People talking. People shouting. The hum of the city.

The frame focuses on a young woman, early 20s. Short, messy bleached hair. A denim jacket over a faded band t-shirt. A tartan skirt. She walks slowly through the crowd on the sidewalk.

"Aqui?"she asks.

Off camera, someone says, "Si."

She stops. She strikes a pose as if part of a photoshoot.

The sky goes dark.

The woman looks up in the sky.

Everyone stops and looks up in the sky.

The world seems to stop.

The noise seems to be put on mute.

"Me siento pesado."

Off camera, "Yo también me siento extraño"

She keeps looking at the sky.

The camera looks up.

A scream goes out from somewhere down the street.

More people start screaming.

Through the sudden darkness in the sky, a form can be made out up in the sky.

The camera zooms towards the object,

fuzzily showing something that looks like a
human being floating in the sky.

LOCATION: MONTSERRAT

DATE: XX/XX/20XX

T.W (CPT). - PRETTY LARGE.

J.K (LT). - NOT A CLUE WHAT IT IS. GOOD VIEW FROM HERE.

T.W. NODS.

J.K. - NOTHING FROM YOUR SIDE THAT HAS ANY INSIGHT??

T.W. - CLASSIFIED.

J.K. - RIGHT BACK AT YOU.

T.W. - I KNOW YOUR TEAM HAS BEEN WATCHING THIS SPACE FOR A TIME NOW, YOU'RE TELLING ME YOU DON'T KNOW WHAT WE'RE LOOKING AT HERE?

J.K. - YOU THINK I'M SITTING ON SOMETHING?

T.W. - I'M FAIRLY CERTAIN YOU ARE SITTING ON SOMETHING, YES

J.K. - AND IF I WAS, WHAT THEN? YOU KNOW HOW THIS WORKS. IT WOULD BE WAY ABOVE MY PAY GRADE AND IF BY SOME MISTAKE THEY DID READ ME IN THEN IT'S UNLIKELY I'D BE SHARING ANY OF THAT WITH YOU.

A LOOK PASSES BETWEEN THEM.

SILENCE FOR A MOMENT. BOTH LOOK UP AT THE SKY, PEERING THROUGH THE DAY TIME SUSPENDED IN SHADOW, TRYING TO MAKE OUT THE DETAIL OF THE BODY.

T.W. - SIGNALS HAS BEEN BUSY. DOESN'T MEAN THEY KNOW ANYTHING BUT COULD BE SOMETHING IN THAT.

J.K. - SIGNALS? THE NERDS ARE GETTING EDGY HUH?

T.W. - THAT COULD BE A WAY OF PUTTING IT. YOUR SIDE HAS EYES UP THERE AND YOU WANT ME TO BELIEVE THAT YOU'RE SEEING NOTHING AND HEARING NOTHING.

J.K. - I don't know what you're wanting from me here, this is what it is and has always been. It's high up enough that we can't get great eyes on it. So it's blurry data and a bunch of the higher ups running around not getting any closer to anything I'd call an answer.

T.W. - Sounds familiar. We haven't heard anything about anyone claiming it.

J.K. - How could they? You think someone owns this? How? You're telling me that somehow, someone, constructed this and then got it up there and no one realised at any point? Where would you even do that?

T.W. - You don't have eyes everywhere.

J.K. - I can tell you we've got enough eyes in enough places that we may as well, and even if we didn't, the blind spot needed for this would be monumental. This is giving me a headache.

A look passes between them.

T.W. - Yeah. We don't have a profile that would come close to fitting this.

J.K. - How could you? This isn't... anything we have priors for.

T.W. - Yeah? You know that? Or we playing guessing games here?

J.K. - Guessing games is all we've got with this.

T.W. - I don't go in for those.

J.K. - I know. But you know who will play those games? The public. As time goes on, and there's nothing coming from any of us on what this is, they're going to get more and more on edge. Once they get themselves to that point, they'll probably line up behind whoever has an idea. Any idea.

T.W. - That's why we need to have cooperation in this.

Stay in our lanes, sure, but all pointing in the same direction. Otherwise, the big guy might go rogue on this.

J.K. - The guy is a maniac.

T.W. - A maniac but one that people get behind when no one else comes up with concrete plans.

They both look at the sky.

T.W. - I wonder if it's going to do anything.

A look passes between them.

David sat in his office. He half-heartedly flipped through papers in front of him. Lectures and notes, scribblings on fig trees and secret gospels. He was distracted, his mind turning to the machine Anna had been talking about. It was madness. Alvin had always been odd. He and Anna would joke about him over dinner. What did Alvin get up to that day? It was a nice comic relief at the end of each day. Or had been.

He couldn't pinpoint why but something about it made his body react. There was tension in him whenever she spoke about it. As though Alvin was designing something that moved into his domain. Or that made Anna think less of him. He had gone to bed, finally, that night and all he could feel was an argument building up inside up that we wanted to let loose on Anna. The next morning it had evaporated but even now, thoughts of this 'model', this 'machine' that Alvin had built. That could tell the future, as if that was a thing. It put him on edge, tense. Ready to shout for... he wasn't sure what.

A light knock at the door.

He looked up and saw Dr. Meriweather, the head of the department. His presence seemed to extend beyond his small stature. He'd known David's father for many years, was largely the reason that David had ended up with the teaching position.

- Tom, I didn't expect you. Did we have something scheduled today?

Tom glanced at the office, the stack of papers. He smiled.

- Clearly. Have you a minute?

- Sure, how can I help?

Tom's brow furrowed for a moment.

- Look, David, we've received a complaint.

David sagged in his seat.

- Sit down. The student in New Testament Studies, I have to

assume? John something? Michaels, wasn't it? He told me he was going to make a complaint.

- Yes, that's him. Seems like a rather… eager, shall I say, student. He claims that the unit is únengaging, aimless', he also suggests that the unit isn't properly engaging with the key text and the assigned readings could offend some.

- So it's not the content they signed up for?

- That seems to be the main thrust of the complaint.

- They had full access to the syllabus ahead of the semester. I know students these days don't spend much time looking at that but if he wanted to know the content it was all there for him.

- I know. But I have to take this seriously, David.

- I know that. But this is frivolous. This isn't about the content, this is about me not being enough of a believer, of his sort of believer to be able to properly deliver this unit… at least in his eyes. You know he came to my service the other week? When he turned up at my office, I think he was probably five words away from calling me a heretic and rounding up a mob. The course is about active critical engagement with the text, it's not about how the text is the divine word. If they wanted apologetics or evangelical cheerleading then this isn't the course for them. He thinks this is the right course being taught the wrong way and he couldn't be further from the truth. It's theology. If we reduced it to what he wants, the whole major would be useless, we may as well just be running a Bible studies course up at Doug's warehouse. He knows Doug by the way, one of those creepy young adults that Doug has surrounding him. I'd guess he's part of their youth pastor program. I have no idea why he is anywhere near our school.

- Calm down. I'm not saying the complaint has any merit or is justified. I agree with you. He's clearly not doing the right course if he isn't going to properly engage with the material.

But we might end up having to mediate this. I'll speak to him and see if I can resolve things. THere is something more to this, a broader point, that I want to talk to you about. He says that it's 'unengaging.' Is there anything that you want to talk about in terms of your approach to teaching recently?

- Mediation. You'll just be giving him a venue to go on a rant at me, at us.

- You're dodging the point, David. Your teaching approach…

David tensed.

- Look. Tom. The course is what it is. This is how I teach it. It's how I've always taught it. I start with the speech on day one to set the scene and then we dig in for a semester. You've never had an issue before. It's always been about critical engagement, asking the hard questions, adjusting their priors and points of view, and pushing back where I need to. There hasn't been a change, except maybe the students. The whole 'I'm here paying you to pass me' mentality rubs me the wrong way. I don't know, maybe that's the game now and I have to change.

- If it's the same course, then why does it feel to me like something is missing?

David frowned.

- Missing? You think I'm not doing my job? You agreed to my hours.

- Not that. I'm asking if you think you're doing your job.

The question hung in the air, sharp and unyielding. David shifted, trying to find the words of an answer.

- I show up. I give the lectures. I keep my office hours. The students aren't just passengers in this, they have to engage with the material, meet it halfway. Even with the mindset of having paid for the course so they should get a pass, I can't do the work for them.

- But do you believe in the material anymore? In what you are trying to teach?

- I... look, you know how it is, Tom. Sometimes the words resonate with you, and other times they are just words. I find... something in the material, and I use that to... I don't know. I feel... I show up and I teach and that's what matters here. Whatever my views on the material are, that doesn't mean the complaint has merit or substance.

- It seems to me that you aren't firing on all cylinders these days. I'm not here to litigate the complaint, I don't really care too much about that, it's just more work I have to deal with. I'm more here because I'm concerned about you. I've never cared whether you have faith. I don't run the department on that. Even when you were younger, a fresh faced pastor, following your fathers path, I didn't care about that because you brought a passion to the material. Your congregants might differ with me on that opinion, I'm sure they would prefer you to be a faithful, devoted soldier of Christ but I just want you to provide insight into the material. Lately it just feels like you're... drifting. I feel it. Your students feel it.

- Drifting isn't a bad word, I guess. But I still teach the unit the way I always have.

- If you are drifting then what are you going to do about it?

- I don't know.

- Look, the other year when you didn't take that grant. I get it, Lisa was too young, though I still think she would have found it as valuable as you.

- But...

- It seems to me that since then you've just been... drifting... away from the material. Away from the students, as though you made the choice that you thought you had to make rather than the right choice, your choice.

- I... Anna was just starting out at the company...

- I know, David, I know. It's like you are starting to go missing, that's the best way I can describe it. I can only imagine that
if your father was still with us that he would be able to see it as
well.

- Don't…

- I'm not saying any of this to upset you but I think you
need to take time. I'm happy if you want to take a sabbatical.
You can focus on your church, put your efforts in there.

- I can teach out the semester and then maybe I can think
through any of that. I guess Lisa is starting to get to an age
where we could maybe think about something like a grant
again.

- It's a time for family now. That thing up there is putting
everyone at edge. The students are coming to talk through
their struggles with it more than they would usually come to
see me.

- Yes, the body. People seem to think that because I'm a
pastor that it means I have some sort of answer to their questions on it.

- Yes yes. If you won't take a sabbatical now, promise me
that with the break at mid-term you go away for a bit, take
Anna and Lisa somewhere and just relax. Recharge. You need
time away from all of this. In the meantime, I'll try and resolve
this situation with Mr. Michaels.

Tom left the office, leaving David to his thoughts. He
looked at his desk. The hum of the office seemed louder than
normal. The windows not holding back the frigid air outside.
He felt heavy.

<hr>

David stood awkwardly in the kitchen, waiting for Anna to
come down.

- Red or white?

He called up the stairs.

- Your choice. It's Kim, she'll drink whatever.

Anna glided down the stairs, a form fitting dress on, her hair up.

- You look nice.

- It's a party.

David tried to hide a sigh.

- I know, I know. We've been doing this long enough, I know you'd prefer not to. But it's Kim. You like Kim. I know she makes you laugh. And it's been a minute since you saw her.

- Who else is going to be there?

- I don't know, a bunch of people, it's a party.

- Anyone from work?

- I think Al is going to be there. I bet he'll want to talk to you about...

David groaned.

The windows of the car fogged up in the unseasonable frost. The mood between them was heavy. Anna looked like she wanted to say something then stopped and then stopped again.

The house loomed large as they approached, up a driveway that took them away from the road and up a hill.

The hum of conversation burbled from behind the door as Anna pressed the doorbell.

- You're going to have fun.

- Maybe we can be here for a bit and then escape early? It would be a shame to waste that dress.

- Wasting the dress would be escaping early. Now have...

Kim opened the door, a large smile threatening to split her face in two as she saw Anna and David.

- You guys! You made it! Come on in! Thanks Dave, I'll take

that. People are in the dining room, and some of the braver souls are out the back on the patio.

Anna took his hand and lead him inside. The weight of his presence was like a suit two sizes too big that he hadn't been able to fit since Anna told him about the dinner.

- I just need to get back into the kitchen but you know most of the people here, go have fun.

Kim scurried off to the kitchen, warm scents coming from that part of the house. Anna walked into the dining room, cozy candlelight illuminating the space. Anna knew how to enter a room. David hovered behind him. People were clumped together in groups at the edges of the room, spilling out into the loungeroom and beyond. The table gleamed with silverware, catching the candlelight as it swayed.

- I'm just going to check if Kim needs any help. I think I can see Al in the loungeroom.

David fought the urge to flee. He put his best face on and moved towards a small group huddled around someone holding a phone. Most preachers were good at moving through crowds, his father had been one of the greats.

He picked up snippets of chatter as he walked towards them.

- … next week is what I heard. Planning some large…

- … they have to do something… try and find out what is going on…

- … over at the base. Says that they'll send a low orbit mission up. Uncrewed of course. Not sure anyone would want to…

He veered away. Next thing they'd be asking for his thoughts on it.

He glimpsed the phone screen showing the neverending shot of the Body.

He walked an arc through the room, not seeing anyone he

wanted to speak to or that were willing to take on new members for their group. Moving into the large loungeroom, he saw Al, back to a wall, a man in his late 20s talking non stop at him. Al looked uncomfortable and bad at hiding it.

David almost laughed. It was the face he often felt he was wearing when Al spoke to him. Though Al's beard and unkempt hair gave it a touch of the uncanny that made him look slightly deranged rather than just put upon by a conversation he didn't want to have. David could just make out what the younger man was saying.

- ... that's the next step you know? Finding that blend between man and machine. I'd love to get your number and chat to you sometime about getting that into my workflow. I work mostly with oils but I saw this guy online a while back that was using robotics to help him paint and it was based on data that had been... something, I mean, you're the data guy right... anyway, it was from his grandmother's old recipe book or something...

A middle aged woman with a kind face appeared out of nowhere. David didn't know who she was.

- You're Anna's David right? She's said so much about you.

- Umm. You have me at a loss.

- Sorry! Of course! I'm Sofia.

- I'm David.

- Of course, silly. I've been working with Anna for about two years now. Well not working 'with' her, I certainly couldn't do the sort of things that her and Alvin and the rest of the team do. I work in the marketing team. Mostly low level campaigns, they don't give me too much work these days. They used to but not really anymore. It's cause I'm part time you see, you know, gotta look after the kids and all that. Oh, you don't have a drink. Do you want a drink?

She gulped down the remainder of her large glass of wine.

- I think they have more wine in the kitchen. Or maybe in the dining room. I should introduce you to my husband. You're a priest right? That's what Anna said you do. That's fascinating. How did you end up doing that? Gary, my husband, well Gary works for a small publishing company. Means he has to work away some of the year and it's just me and the kids but it's what he loves and he's good at it. I think he is. You ever think about whether your husband. Not your husband, your partner, cause you've got a wife. You ever think about whether they are any good at what they do for a job? Or if they just do that job because that's the job they have. Gary loves books. Loves them. You should see our house. Bookshelves everywhere. But I don't know that means that he's any…

David pretended to have been called over by Alvin. He nodded his head and made to move away.

- Sorry, I think I just saw Alvin call me over. I've been meaning to talk to him about something.

- Oh, Alvin. You know he's a genius. I've never met anyone quite like him.

David wandered away, past Alvin and the young artist and towards the back of the house. On the patio, people sat under a heater, blankets thrown over their laps. They chattered and smiled and laughed. David went outside and stood at the railing of the patio, looking out at the night sky. He missed smoking on nights like these. The smell would bring him back to his father. The scent of Port Royale tobacco, his father puffing on the pipe that had a carving of his face. The night smelled cold, punctuated with wafts of strawberry and kiwi vape.

No one noticed him standing there, or if they did they chose not to bother him. People slowly moved inside as the temperature dropped further. His breath blew mist. A light dusting of snow began to drift in.

Lost in thoughts, he felt the railing sag with the weight of someone. He turned to find Alvin standing there, a good humoured smile hanging on his face. He put two glasses of amber liquid on the railing.

- Saw you in there pinned down by Sofia, thought you might like a drink. Takes a bit to get over an ambush from her.

David grabbed one of the glasses and lightly clinked it against the other.

- Thanks. I saw you were ambushed by something as well.

- Some kid. Figure he has to be one of Kim's collection. Think he said something about being shown in her gallery.

They took a beat. Silence hung between them.

- I wanted to talk to you about something, Dave.

David flinched. There were people he let call him 'Dave', Alvin was not on that list.

- I'm sure Anna has told you what I've been working on.

- She has.

- And that it predicted the figure.

- She mentioned but I don't think I believe it.

- I'm not sure I believe it. I built this thing and now it's like it's its own thing. A being almost.

David could feel a flash of tension run through him.

- I'm thinking that I'm going to go out and start up my own company. If the bosses find out that I've created this thing, and on their time no less, then I can't see how they won't fire me. Not even with everything I've done for them over the years They won't care about…

- Not sure why you wanted to tell me about this, Alvin.

- Well, I want Anna to come with me. She's critical to me being able to move this into production. I'd probably try and get some of the rest of the team but Anna is the one that I need if it's all going to work.

- Sure seems like a conversation to have with her.

- I haven't talked to her about it yet. You know how it can be with startups…

- Not really but sure.

- Well, chances are if Anna came with me then she wouldn't draw a salary for at least a few months. Thought it would be worth talking to you about that. Obviously you've got a job at the college and you preach, so I'm sure you guys would be fine but…

- And there's Lisa.

- Lisa, yeah. A kid isn't nothing you know.

- I don't know what to tell you Alvin, it's a question for Anna. Though if you go, or get fired, then that would probably mean that Anna could actually head up the development team rather than sharing it with you.

- Well, yeah, I guess that might happen. Would be up to the bosses. If she didn't come then maybe they'd do that. But she's wasted there. She's so much more than they let her be. This is the real deal too. This could be something that changes everything.

- You wouldn't be the first one to think that.

- This is different, Dave. Dave. Listen. This didn't just predict the figure appearing in the sky. This has predicted things that are a year out from now. It's predicting things for later tonight. Everything its predicted up to this point, at least with a high degree of certainty, has happened. All the turmoil on the markets since the figure appeared, it's gotten down to the individual security level. The fact that they've started evacuating parts of Spain, it predicted that weeks ago and to the individual town and city level. This is something else.

David felt tense. A feeling like rage coursing through him. He wanted to hit Alvin. He wanted to pummel his stupid face. He needed to get this aggression out. He wasn't sure where the sensation came from.

- The future doesn't exist, Alvin. And a computer can't tell what is going to happen.

- I know it sounds crazy…

- You're right, you do sound crazy.

- I get it, I get it. With what you do, this must seem like some sort of blasphemy.

Maybe it did, maybe that's what this was. David might have found himself adrift but something like this pushed against him, everything he had made himself care about and believe in a way that frustrated him. No. Enraged him. This feeling was a response to a direct attack on himself. Who he was. Alvin's voice became muffled and he worked to hide his anger from his face. The one time he'd ever seen his father swear at someone was as a child at an extended family gathering. An uncle of his had been mouthing off something about how First Nations peoples were handed everything and didn't have to work a day in their lives. A real 'up-by-your-boot-straps' type that believed in the Dream in a way that never resonated with David. He hadn't seen, or heard, the whole conversation but the next thing he knew his father was standing up from the table with a loud clatter, thrusting his chair into the side of the table so the plates rattled and with one of his large fingers pointing dead straight at his uncle said "You don't know what the fuck you are talking about." David and his mother found him out of the car, still fuming, hours later when they left the gathering.

Anna walked out onto the patio. Her grin betrayed that she was a few drinks in already.

- Ah, my two husbands.

David grimaced.

- Lighten up, babe. Come on. Everyone is inside, we're going to have dinner. You should see the spread that Kim has prepared.

–

Braised Short Ribs with Red Wine Reduction
Serves: 20
Prep Time: 45 minutes
Cook Time: 4 hours
Rest Time: 15 minutes
Ingredients
For the Short Ribs:

- 20 bone-in beef short ribs (approximately 15–18 lbs)
- Salt and freshly ground black pepper (generous amounts)
- 6 tbsp vegetable oil (for searing, divided into batches)
- 3 large yellow onions, diced
- 6 medium carrots, diced
- 6 celery stalks, diced
- 8 garlic cloves, minced
- 6 tbsp tomato paste
- 6 cups dry red wine (Cabernet Sauvignon or Merlot works well)
- 8 cups beef stock (plus more if needed)
- 6 sprigs fresh thyme
- 6 sprigs fresh rosemary
- 4 bay leaves

For the Root Vegetables:

- 4 lbs parsnips, peeled and cut into chunks
- 4 lbs baby potatoes, halved
- 4 lbs carrots, peeled and cut into large pieces
- 4 tbsp olive oil
- Salt and freshly ground black pepper (to taste)

- 2 tsp dried thyme

For Garnish:

- ½ cup fresh parsley, finely chopped

Instructions
1. Sear the Short Ribs

1. Preheat the oven to 325°F (160°C).
2. Pat the short ribs dry with paper towels and season generously with salt and pepper.
3. Heat 2–3 large Dutch ovens or heavy-bottomed oven-safe pots over medium-high heat. Divide the vegetable oil among the pots.
4. Working in batches, sear the short ribs on all sides until browned, about 4 minutes per side. Remove and set aside.

2. Build the Flavor Base

1. Reduce the heat to medium and divide the diced onions, carrots, and celery among the pots. Sauté until softened, about 5–7 minutes.
2. Stir in the garlic and tomato paste, cooking for an additional 2 minutes.

3. Deglaze and Add Liquid

1. Pour 2 cups of red wine into each pot, scraping the bottom to release any browned bits (fond). Simmer for 5 minutes to reduce slightly.

2. Return the short ribs to the pots and divide the beef stock, thyme, rosemary, and bay leaves evenly among them. The liquid should almost cover the ribs.

4. Braise in the Oven

1. Cover the pots with tight-fitting lids and transfer to the preheated oven. Braise for 3.5–4 hours, rotating the pots halfway through if necessary. Add more beef stock if the liquid reduces too much.
2. The short ribs are done when the meat is tender and pulls away from the bone.

5. Prepare the Root Vegetables

1. While the ribs braise, toss the parsnips, baby potatoes, and carrots with olive oil, salt, pepper, and thyme in a large mixing bowl.
2. Spread the vegetables on 2–3 large baking sheets in an even layer.
3. Roast in the oven at 400°F (200°C) for 40–50 minutes, tossing halfway through, until caramelized and tender.

6. Finish the Sauce

1. Remove the short ribs from the pots and cover with foil to keep warm.
2. Strain the braising liquid from each pot through a fine mesh sieve into a large saucepan or stockpot, discarding the solids. Simmer over medium heat to

reduce by half, about 15–20 minutes, until thickened. Skim off excess fat if necessary.

7. Serve

1. Arrange the short ribs on large platters with the roasted root vegetables around them. Drizzle the red wine reduction generously over the ribs and vegetables.
2. Garnish with fresh parsley and a touch of paprika and serve immediately.

—

David poked at the food that had been served to them. The guests chattered excitedly. Anna was up near the head of the table, close to Kim. He always felt like he was floating when she wasn't close to him.

His company for the dinner portion of the evening was Sofia from earlier. Her husband, Gary, didn't seem to be too far from her. They'd been introduced and there was little in common except that Gary worked in the world of books and David had to read books so he could do his job. Sofia was the sort that would talk through a hurricane, a never ending blizzard of words coming out of her mouth. He guessed that was the nature of marketing types, though he found little of it interesting and kept taking top ups when offers of more drinks came past.

Anna was in her element. She'd look over and smile with warmth from time to time. This was her at her best. David felt blessed that he'd met her all those years ago. Sweet, kind, brilliant. Despite her intellect, she wasn't reserved in the way that people assumed when they were told she worked on deep machine learning models. In the way people assumed some pious milquetoast when they heard David was a pastor (and perhaps they were right), people assumed that Anna was the sort that bled into the wallpaper and would talk math at them all night if given the chance. But Anna, she commanded most rooms she walked into. He wondered if Alvin would have been given half the chances he had if not for Anna. Anna, who would make you laugh and swear like a sailor.

David drank heavily. It helped to tune Sofia's words into a slightly less annoying buzz. Her words fading in and out as he listened to other conversation happening at the table. Most seemed to be talking about the Body, which was no surprise given it was all that most could talk about these days. He was surprised there wasn't a screen playing in the corner of the room reminding everyone of its presence.

The young artist was talking about its impact on his work.

David couldn't hear Anna and Kim but they were laughing.

A cluster of people near him started to theorise on the nature of the body. David drank heavily.

- A quantum projection. That's what I read the other day.

- What does that even mean?

Gary, Sofia's husband was speaking.

- The way I understand it is it's a physical representation from a higher dimension that has crossed into the dimensions we can perceive.

- That doesn't make any sense, I don't understand what you're saying.

- We have a number of quite respected scientists that write for us. Well, for one of our imprints that publishes a lot of university research. The way I had it described to me is that there's a larger number of dimensions than what we can perceive. We can perceive three dimensions, that's space and we feel the effect of four dimensions, that's time, but we can't really perceive it.

People had paused eating the succulent meat and stared at Gary as he went on.

- Imagine for a second that you live in a place that's only two dimensions. Like a picture on a piece of paper. You can't see outside of that piece of paper right? That's the whole world. Now, let's say that a three dimensional object gets placed on the paper, your world. Like this glass. How are you going to see that?

- Well, it's a glass, so it looks like a glass. But I guess I'm really small cause I exist on a piece of paper so the glass looks giant? Is that what you're getting at?

- No. That's not it. When the glass gets put down, you just see the lines on the edges of the glass that touch the paper. Because that's all your world is, it's all two dimensions. So you can't see the whole. But we can see the whole glass because we can perceive that extra dimension. That's what's happening with the Body. It's how we're perceiving something being pushed onto our dimension. What we're seeing is just what we can perceive of it rather than all of it.

No one knew what to say to any of that. For a moment a number of people went to say something, their mouths flapping open for a second and then closing. A man David didn't know was the first to speak.

- Nonsense. That doesn't make sense.

The young artist, his words loose with drink, spoke.

- You know crop circles? I heard that's what crop circles are. Some higher dimensional being pushing through our dimension and leaving a scar.

Gary looked annoyed that he hadn't been realised for the learned scholar he believed himself to be.

- Well, what do you think it is then?

David slurred out a response.

- No one knows.

Gary looked at him coolly.

- I'm surprised you don't have an answer, pastor. Isn't that the whole thing with the church?

- If you want to play it that way, I'm sure there are all manner of priests you can find that would give you certainty and answers. I've heard it's the second coming. I've been told it's the sign before the end times, calling us to repent. My local bartender thinks it's a hologram. I don't know. None of us do. It's a thought. It's up there. It's doing something, or it's not. I saw the other day they're planning some mission up to it to see what it is.

- We all saw that.

David spilled a drop or two of whiskey from his glass. The table cloth soaked it up. His hand movements were getting erratic.

- Right, so then we'll have a sense of what it could be, until then it's all just noise and wasted breath. If you need to pray then pray, if you want to wax lyrical about it being some quantum perception or whatever you said then go for your life but I don't know and neither do you.

A silence fell on the cluster of people. Most turned their attention to their dinner and recommenced eating. David could feel Gary's eyes on him as he drank and drank again.

THE GHOST of dinner slammed into the toilet bowl, acid howling up David's throat. He kneeled in front of the toilet and heaved. A sweating prayer to whatever God he once felt so close to. Sweat cooled quickly on his brow in the cold air coming from the exhaust fan. His body screamed at him, trying to get everything out. The world blurred. His body paused for a second and he wondered if he was done.

He watched, eyes sagging heavily, as a cockroach wandered into the bathroom. He stared at it, its antennae substituting for eyes, feeling its way across the cool floor. He lay down next to the toilet and kept watching as the roach moved closer and closer to him. His stomach continued to roil, forcing him up and over the toilet again, barely making it in time as a long stream spewed from his mouth, vomit splashing up from the water in the toilet and a small chunk hitting the floor.

Staring down into the toilet bowl, he saw nothing but red. The remnants of dinner and it's too rich sauce, little misshapen cubes of potato illuminated by the bright deep scarlet liquid.

The roach moved over to the small chunk on the floor and felt its dimensions.

David lay back down and watched.

A small knock came at the door. Anna's voice drifted into the bathroom.

- Babe, are you alright in there?

David gurgled a response that tried to tell her to come in. He saw two Anna's come into the room and lean down to look at him.

- We'll get out of here. I can't believe you drank this much.

- You remember when we were younger and we'd go out to the desert? We should do that again.

- Right. Sure. Yeah, definitely. Can you stand? I need to get you to the car. I can't believe you drank so much you vomited. What are you a teenager? I'd expect this from Lisa but come on David, you're a grown ass man.

David gurgled, embarrassed but too drunk to properly register it. He tried to lift himself to his feet. The roach scurried away as he moved.

– Like Charlie Brown?

– Yeah, you know that womp womp.

– Always sounds like a sad trombone under water.

– Like that. That's how I hear them these days. All womp womp and words fading into the background. I don't know if I've had a proper conversation with my dad in years.

– I like your dad. He doesn't say much but he always seems nice.

– Yeah well, he doesn't like you. Thinks you're a bad influence on me or something.

– Sure, sure. Little does he realise all the things you got me into.

Lisa, Rachel and Brody huddled in the cool night air. Most blew from their mouths as they spoke.

– What can I say? You always get away with more when you're the kid of a preacher man.

– That first time I got properly actually high. When I thought i could taste the sound of the dashboard in that car that guy... what was his name? That senior that always crushed on eighth graders? He drove us around all night and you thought we'd been kidnapped.

– Pillman was the guy. That was me got you that high that night.

– I know.

– Don't you forget it, kid.

Brody looked at the girls with an excited look on his face.

– So what'll be tonight? What's the game?

Lisa tapped her chin deep in mock thought.

– Traffic.

– Traffic!

Brody shouted into the night air, an explosion of his breath visible. Rachel laughed and cuddled into him.

– Megan coming?

– I assume so, she should be here sometime soon.

Rachel grabbed at Lisa's side.

– No wonder you want to play Traffic. Wanting to get Megan down to her delicates huh.

– I mean, I'm not going to complain. Point is, i want to feel something.

Brody leered.

– Bet you do.

The three of them started to undress. Slowly peeling away each layer to allow time to adjust as the breeze caressed their flesh. Hazy fluorescent light illuminated the asphalt of the car park.

Brody jumped from foot to foot, now down to his underwear, while the girls continued undressing. Megan's voice called out across the parking lot.

– The game is Traffic!

Lisa turned and smiled at Megan strode towards them. There was a confidence in her step that Lisa tried her hardest to mimic whenever she could. She knew it didn't work how she wanted. She kept her eyes fixed, a smile crinkling the corner of her eyes, as she continued undressing.

Megan's large boots crunched on the ground as she made it over to them. Mischief in her eyes, she quickly started getting her clothes off.

– Don't tell me we're just going down to our knickers. I thought we were playing Traffic, not some Fisher Price My First running shit.

Lisa looked at Rachel and Brody. Rachel grinned. Brody looked unsure. Lisa unhooked her bra and started taking her panties off. Brody gasped.

– She's actually doing it.

Rachel elbowed him in the side and started stripping down as well. Megan laughed.

– Not sure anyone really wants to see what you're hiding, Brody but best get on with it.

All four stood naked, the air running over their bodies. They slowly made their way over to the road, Rachel pushed up against the side of Brody for warmth. The light from the parking lot dimmer this close to the road. The overgrown grass swaying against their ankles.

Megan was the first to speak.

– Who's up?

No one made to step forward. Finally, Lisa spoke up.

– I guess it's me.

– Well assume the position!

Lisa crouched down, ready to spring into action. She felt tense and excited. Fire accelerated through her veins. Her body aching to move, everything trying to hold it back. The road was dark, the night quiet. Megan moved around behind her and covered her eyes with a blindfold. She could hear the other three slowly move back from the edge of the road. Further down the road she could hear the distant rumble of a car. She breathed in deep.

A beat.

A beat.

Her heart, trying to rip through her chest it was beating so loud.

A shout from Megan.

– Go!

Lisa's legs pushed her forward from the grass at the side of the road. Her feet pounding on the aged road, the sole of her foot crunching on kicked up stones, the rough asphalt tearing into her heels.

She ran.

She ran.

A car horn could be heard, blaring at her. The sound of tires squealing as a car moved erratically, trying to maneuver around this flash of flesh that had darted out in front of it in the inky black of the night. Adrenaline coursed through her, exploded every fibre of her, making her nerve endings crackle and come to life. She felt the movement of air that could only mean the car missing her by inches. A muffled shout dragging from somewhere beyond her. She kept running, she kept running until her feet felt the grass on the other side and she threw herself on to the ground in long cold grass. Removing the blindfold, she crawled over to a nearby clump of bushes and lay down. Her breathing ragged, she stared up at the sky and slowly traced patterns on her skin with her fingers, her skin crackling with electricity, not yet sated.

From beyond the road she heard a whoop. Tires squealed to a halt further down the road. Silence. The car idled. For a moment Lisa thought the car might come back but then it drove off into the night. More cheering came from beyond the road.

After they'd all gone across and lay there, trying to catch their breath and trying to pull Rachel and Brody apart, their hands on each other in a way neither Lisa or Megan wanted to be around, and after they'd got dressed again, they made their way into a field. The dark of night fully set in, the lack of streetlights meaning the sky was awash in stars. The only sounds, the distant rumble of the odd car and the chirrup of crickets.

Brody stood, his neck craned up to the sky. Watching, unmoved, he didn't speak. Rachel lay back on the grass, trying to mimic the crickets softly.

Lisa sat, her legs crossed. Lightly picking at grass. Megan gently rested her head on Lisa's shoulder, the sort of thing that made Lisa never know what to do with her hands. Megan shuffled around and lay back with her head in Lisa's lap. She looked up at Lisa with those sparkling eyes that made Lisa gulp. A defiance in the stare. Lisa looked right back. Megan broke the gaze and looked over at Brody.

– You can't see it from here.

– I know. But it's up there, somewhere. I reckon I can feel it.

– Yeah.

– Like heavy.

– Yeah. Heavy.

Rachel chirruped.

Lisa leaned down and lightly brushed hair from Megan's forehead. Megan smiled. Lisa felt like her skin was too big.

– I ever tell you about when I was a kid?

Lisa shook her head. Megan would do this in the afterglow of the games. Always so casual, so cool that it hurt, she'd tell secrets in those moments after they'd pushed themselves and were alive and the colour wasn't turned down.

– My folks got me into it. I was one of those kids you see on socials. Had my own channel and everything. I guess cause I'm an only child and they wanted to make sure they had a way of properly interacting with me or something. I don't know. It was like mass manufactured parenting. Anytime we'd pay would just be for the cameras. I mean, when I was fairly young I thought it was great, you get big enough and you get free stuff all the time and we went all sorts of places because places want you to come and play with their stuff cause then other kids will buy it. Did it for years and years. My earliest memories are of making that stuff, stupid little videos and I'm sure those first memories when my parents started doing it with me, just what I can remember. I even came up with this 'la la la' thing, I can probably still do it.

– That's cute. Little social star.

– It wasn't cute at all. It was demented. Just this walking, talking advertisement. Everything was about getting clicks and selling a product. If a run of videos wasn't getting as many views as my parents thought it should, I'd hear them arguing at night after I'd gone to bed about what they should do to change things up and how they were going to get enough people watching again. It's how they made their money. I'm pretty sure it's why they split up. Like they'd spent so much energy focused on me and all this video stuff, except not really on me except as like a worker for them, then one day they realised they hadn't spent any time on themselves or even who they were anymore and just didn't want to be together anymore. Except they kept working together doing these trashy videos with me cause that's what they did now. And they'd pat themselves on the back cause even though they weren't together anymore they'd tell people they'd found a way to stay friends through it all and wasn't it so good for me. I found out a couple of years ago that they'd sell photos of me, nothing sketchy but still, to people who called themselves my fans on socials. It was gross.

    – So why'd you stop?

    – Got sick of it, stopped being fun, didn't want to. Stopped being cute.

---

*BROTHERS AND SISTERS, the time for passive faith has ended! The figure in the sky—the vast, unyielding body that looms above Europe is not merely a sign, it is a **warning**. For months it has hung there, dark and silent, a monument to the spiritual truth we can no longer ignore: Spain, this once-mighty land of Gospel proclamation, is now under the shadow of Satan's dominion.*

*   I do not say this lightly. This is a call to arms. For the figure in the sky is God's trumpet blast, declaring to His people that the battle is raging and the hour is late. Spain has become a battlefield—a land*

under siege by the forces of darkness. But I declare to you today, in the name of Jesus Christ: **that land will not belong to Satan! That land will not fall to his lies! The Lord has sent His sign to awaken His people and to reclaim what is His!**

Why has this immense body chosen Spain as its place of manifestation? The answer is both sobering and clear: Spain has become a stronghold for Satan's schemes.

This is not just a land—it is a spiritual gateway, a crossroads where cultures and faiths have collided for centuries. Once a bastion of Christian power, a land that sent missionaries to the ends of the earth, Spain has now been overrun by secularism, moral decay, filth and rebellion against God. The figure in the sky is a divine declaration that the enemy's forces have entrenched themselves there, and they are waging war not only against Spain, not only against this world, not only against Christian's across the land but against the Kingdom of God itself.

Let us not be deceived! This figure is not simply a celestial phenomenon—it is a **spiritual map,** *showing us where the enemy has concentrated his forces. Spain, under the shadow of this body, has become a symbol of the enemy's dominion. But hear this, hear it now: it is also a symbol of the victory to come! For God has not sent this sign to paralyse us with fear, but to ignite the church, His church, with holy fire!*

Brothers and sisters, this is not a time for complacency. We are at war! This is not a war of flesh and blood, but a spiritual war against the forces of darkness that seek to destroy our nation and deceive the world.

Ephesians 6:12 tells us:

"For we wrestle not against flesh and blood, but against principalities, against powers, against the rulers of the darkness of this world, against spiritual wickedness in high places."

The body in the sky is a **manifestation of these spiritual forces,** *these principalities and powers, a silent testament to the* *enemy's grip on that land. But let me remind you: Satan is a defeated foe. His power is real, but it is not ultimate. The battle belongs to the Lord, and we are His chosen soldiers to reclaim this territory for His Kingdom!*

Secularism has overtaken the land. Morality has crumbled. The truth of the Gospel has been rejected, and false ideologies have taken root. Spain, once a lighthouse of faith, is now a stronghold of the enemy.

And yet, God has not abandoned this land! The figure in the sky is a declaration that the war is not over. Satan may have claimed Spain for his purposes, but God's people will not stand idly by. This is our call to arms, our moment to rise and fight, to don our armour of God and go forth into battle.

Brothers and sisters, what is our response to this sign? How do we fight against the forces of Satan that have entrenched themselves in Spain and beyond? The answer is found in the Word of God:

Repentance as Our Weapon: The first step in any holy war is repentance. The church must cleanse itself of compromise, confess its sins, and stand pure before the Lord. If we are to fight the forces of Satan, we must first ensure that we are fully aligned with God's will.

Prayer as Our Power: Prayer is the weapon that shakes the heavens. Let us cry out for Spain, for its people, and for its deliverance from Satan's grip. Let us pray for revival, for the breaking of strongholds, and for the Holy Spirit to sweep through this nation with power! We will pray and we will pray and we will not cease until the enemy lays before us.

Spiritual Warfare as Our Duty: The enemy's grip on Spain is not just cultural or political—it is spiritual. We must engage in spiritual warfare, tearing down the strongholds of darkness through fasting, worship, and the proclamation of God's truth.

Unity as Our Strength: Satan fears a united church. Let us set aside our divisions and stand as one body, united under the banner of Christ, to confront the enemy's schemes.

But let me speak plainly: this battle begins with you. If there is sin in your life, if there is compromise in your heart, you are not ready for this war. The figure in the sky is not only a sign for Spain — it is a sign for you. It is calling you to repentance, to holiness, to surrender.

Do not wait another day! The time is short, and the stakes are eternal. The body in the sky is a reminder that Satan is real, that his forces are advancing, but also that God's victory is assured for those who stand with Him.

Revelation 3:2 commands us:

"Wake up! Strengthen what remains and is about to die, for I have found your deeds unfinished in the sight of my God."

Wake up, church! Wake up, warriors of God! The battle is raging, and the time to act is now.

Brothers and sisters, do not fear. Though the figure in the sky may seem overwhelming, though the forces of Satan may seem unstoppable, we know the truth: **Christ has already won the victory!** *The cross has defeated the powers of sin and death, and the empty tomb proclaims that Satan's reign is temporary and doomed.*

Revelation 12:11 declares:

"They triumphed over him by the blood of the Lamb and by the word of their testimony; they did not love their lives so much as to shrink from death."

This is our victory cry! The blood of Jesus has broken every chain, and the Word of God is our sword in this holy war. Let us stand firm, knowing that the enemy's strongholds will crumble before the power of our God.

The figure in the sky is a line in the sand. It challenges us. Will we stand with God and fight for His Kingdom, or will we cower in fear and allow Satan to claim what does not belong to him?

Let us rise as warriors of the Most High! Let us take up the weapons of prayer, fasting, and faith, and let us march boldly into this battle. Spain will not belong to Satan. The enemy's dominion will not endure. For the Lord has spoken, and His church will prevail!

Heavenly Father, we cry out to You today. Forgive us for our complacency. Strengthen us for the battle ahead. Break the strongholds over Spain, and raise up Your army to reclaim this land for Your glory. We declare victory in the name of Jesus, and we commit ourselves fully to Your holy war. Amen and amen!

Rise, church of God! The battle is here, and the victory is ours!

Mysterious Colossal Humanoid Appears in Earth's Stratosphere, Governments and Scientists Scramble for Answers

By David Langford
October 12, 20XX

WASHINGTON, D.C. — In an event unlike any other in recorded history, a towering, humanoid figure—spanning an estimated 160 kilometers from head to toe—has appeared in Earth's stratosphere. Hovering motionless, it lies just beneath the edge of space, casting a shadow over vast portions of the surface below. Its presence is unnervingly static, leaving governments, scientists, and the public grappling with the implications of this mysterious and unexplained occurrence.

A Global Puzzle Unfolds

The figure, eerily human in form, first appeared high in the sky over Europe, with its outline soon being confirmed by satellite imagery and ground observations. It wasn't long before the immensity of the figure became clear—stretching across the sky as if frozen in place. While its surface appears organic and smooth, its composition remains unknown.

Initial reports suggested the figure was in geosynchronous orbit, but further analysis revealed that it hovers within Earth's stratosphere, approximately 50 kilometers above the surface. This is an altitude typically reserved for high-altitude balloons and the upper limits of weather phenomena—now home to something so vast it defies understanding.

Global Reactions

Governments across the world are scrambling to respond to this unprecedented situation. "We are treating this as a matter of global importance," the White House said. "We do not yet understand what this figure is, where it came from, or whether it poses any threat to humanity. But we are working tirelessly to find answers."

In New York, the United Nations convened an emergency session to address the figure's sudden appearance. Leaders from spacefaring nations pledged cooperation in the investigation. "This is an event that transcends borders and touches on the very fabric of our understanding of the world," said UN Secretary-General Angela Lo. "Global cooperation is essential in unraveling this mystery."

Some governments, particularly those in regions directly under the figure's shadow, have issued precautionary advisories, asking citizens to remain indoors during certain periods. Chairman of the U.S. Joint Chiefs of Staff, confirmed that the military is monitoring the situation closely. "While we are prepared for any eventuality, there is no indication that the figure is hostile," he said, stressing that military experts remain in constant contact with scientists assessing the situation.

Theories and Speculation

The humanoid form of the figure has prompted a wide range of theories. Some suggest extraterrestrial origins, while others point to the possibility of an advanced technological creation, potentially by a previously unknown civilization. Still others favor more metaphysical interpretations, viewing the figure as a divine or symbolic entity.

However, scientists are urging caution in speculating about the figure's origin or purpose. "We simply don't have enough information yet," said Dr. Elena Moreau. "What we need right now is more data—hard facts. Speculation at this point only muddies the waters."

One of the biggest mysteries is how the figure appeared so suddenly and in such a precise location. "It's difficult to fathom how an object of this size could arrive without any prior detection," said Dr. Vikram Patel, a lead astronomer with the European Space Agency. "There were no warnings—nothing. This suggests either highly advanced technology or phenomena we've never encountered."

Some scientists have noted that the figure's stratospheric position, which keeps it in a quasi-stationary state relative to Earth's surface, might suggest it was "placed" intentionally. Others caution against assuming it was created by intelligent life, stressing that the universe can produce strange anomalies that defy easy explanation.

A Growing Anxiety

As the world waits for more definitive answers, anxiety is spreading. Conspiracy theories are multiplying, with some speculating that the figure is a harbinger of global disaster or the result of a secret military experiment gone awry. Others fear it could signal first contact with an extraterrestrial species—or worse, an invasion.

However, the figure's presence is already having tangible effects on Earth. In regions under its vast shadow, the temperature has dropped, and unusual weather patterns have begun to emerge. These effects are localized for now, but scientists worry about the long-term impacts on the climate if the figure remains where it is.

Stock markets have also felt the pressure, with volatility spiking as investors weigh the global economic consequences of the figure's appearance. Meanwhile, travel disruptions are becoming more common, with aviation authorities rerouting flights to avoid passing directly under the figure.

A Historic Moment

For many, the figure's sudden appearance signals a turning point in human history. "This is not just a scientific enigma—it's a cultural and existential moment," said Dr. Moreau. "It challenges our understanding of our place in the cosmos."

As humanity looks to the sky, the unanswered question remains: What does this mean for us? Is this the beginning of a new era, or simply a momentary anomaly? With each passing day, the figure looms larger in the global consciousness, even as its purpose remains elusive.

Next Steps

NASA and other international space agencies are reportedly preparing a series of exploratory missions to observe the figure more closely. However, launching missions into the stratosphere presents significant technical challenges. "This is uncharted territory, literally and figuratively," explained Dr. Patel. "We need to be cautious as we attempt to investigate something this enormous in such a precarious part of the atmosphere."

For now, the world watches and waits. The figure remains suspended, silent and unyielding, as humanity struggles to comprehend what it is—and what it may mean for our future.

Reporting contributed by Julia Maddox in London, Ahmed Nasr in Cairo, and Li Wei in Beijing.

Blinding lights and swooping cameras. David sat high in the auditorium and watched the spectacle take place below and around him. The thumping music, the people standing, hands outstretched to the sky as the band on stage played a non offensive rock ballad expressing their worship.

Doug, portly and his hair more grey than David remembered, sauntered out on to stage. The crowd cheered at the sight of him. David felt himself momentarily swept away, the scene created to wash over, to press down on Doug's flock. A mass psychogenic fugue state, some mass hypnosis. David shook himself out of it and blanched, this wasn't what this should be.

Doug launched into his sermon, the flock murmuring as he spoke of powers and principalities and Satan's dominion. The body, the body. Doug thundered and raved, he whispered and brought this crowd close. He gave them orders and sent them on their missions as soldiers in the army of the Lord. He prayed, he spat, he was taken by the spirit and brought forth words in tongues.

David was bored.

The crowd shouted amen.

The people around David were swept away in the presence of Doug.

Doug, sweating and his body shaking, told them to feel the power of the Lord. People shook and fell to their knees. Demons were cast out and ailments cured.

The congregation were spent, they made their way out to the lobby to shake Doug's hand and head out into the world, healed and ready for another week of keeping the devil at bay.

David lingered, hoping to catch Doug. The crowd thinned, after a time, leaving Doug beaming and nearly alone in the lobby. David went up and softly said hello. Doug, never one to speak at anything below his preaching volume, boomed.

- David! Shaffley, this here is Pastor Hale. He runs the little church, you know, the one on the hill.

His colleague shook his hand, gave him a look over, a grimace and then shuffled off.

- You've finally come to see how it's done? Good man. Good man. Do you have time to chat?

- I can stay for a bit. It's certainly a show you put on…

- 3 times a week and twice on Sunday. Of course, this is the big one, the one I always make sure I preach. I have junior ministers that I use for the other ones.

- I noticed the cameras…

- Well, we are syndicated now. Managed to sell off the back catalogue of sermons, quite a bit of money that we put towards expanding the flock.The Sunday sermon goes wide and then we have smaller distribution on the other sermons through the week.

Doug started walking off, leaving David to follow after him like some sort of dog, like when they were younger. He trailed him to his office, too big and a resounding view of the too big car park.

- How can I help?

Doug leaned back in his chair.

- I have one of your kids in my class. Or at least, I can only assume he's one of yours. He certainly would be your sort.

- Oh yes. John. He's been a core part of the youth ministry for a couple of years now.

- If he's part of the youth ministry then why is he bothering with my class?

- Hell if I know. Not sure he'd get much of anything out of it. He's been telling me all about what you've been saying at that university of yours. That belief isn't a prerequisite, that it's about history and archeology and critical analysis.

His voice had a dismissive sing-song to it.

- That's what a university level theology course is, of course.

- Garbage is what it is. I have my doctorate you know, from an actual university that actually teaches theology, not the blasphemous rubbish you teach.

- This is all incredibly cynical what you're doing here. The lights and the spectacle. The casting out of demons like you're a prophet.

- We are prophets here! We are the new church! What do you have?

- My morals. I haven't sold out for money. All this fire and brimstone and end of days…

- Your father preached like this. Everyone knew the spirit ran through him. He made people feel something, he brought them closer to the Lord. He prayed and he shook the devil. He'd be disgusted to see what his son turned out to be.

- How dare you!

- How dare I? How dare you? Your father is why I became a preacher. I wasn't a good kid, you'd remembered but through him I heard the call of the Lord. Your father is how I was touched by Jesus and came to know him. Now you come to me because what? Because some kid, who will become a great preacher, is calling you out when you are trying to sell your heresy. What happened to you? You were never going to be one of the greats but you knew the Lord. Your sermons always were pretty dull, that's right, but you had a congregation and they came to the Lord through you. Now what? I know most of your flock have ended up coming here.

- At least I'm preaching for the right reasons? You just do it to get money. You're a charlatan. All the theatre of people falling to their knees. You are everything wrong with the church.

David rose to his feet. Rage coursing through his body, his muscles quaking.

- We are called to preach the word of the Lord and we are called to expand our flock until the world can be saved. That's what I'm doing, David. Everything else is just noise. Especially now, with that abomination hanging in the sky!

- You don't know what that is. It could be anything. It's not what you say it is.

- And you don't know either. I look up and I see a clear sign of the Adversary's mark and I will do everything to make sure that this world does not fall to his influence. I'm going to put on my armor of God and I am going to pray and we will win. I feel sorry for you that you can't see that. Look to the word of the Lord, it is all there. The signs are there in the book. It is there in Daniel 7:13, in Revelation 6:12-14. We are living through the prophesied age. All this filth that you support because you say you know Christ. You know nothing and if we were to follow you we would be lead to ruin.

David wanted to lash out, to throw punches. God he wanted to feel Doug's nose break under his fist. But he didn't, he just stared at him and then walked away.

- That's what I thought.

TIMESTAMP: 20XX-04-11 14:37:02 UTC
Model Confidence Threshold: 99.8%
Key Predictions:

1. **Individual Level:**
   - *Subject ID #2073F4:* Will change residence to Latitude 40.7128° N, Longitude 74.0060° W within 34 days.
   - *Subject ID #99AC32:* Likelihood of significant health event (cardiovascular): 87.3% within 6 weeks.
   - *Subject ID #EFA941:* Predicted to publish widely discussed academic paper titled "The Quantum Body: Theoretical Impacts of the Sky Figure" by 20XX-03-15.
2. **Regional Level:**
   - Meteorological anomalies projected over southern Spain beginning 20XX-05-01, extending for 12 days. Precipitation will deviate +450% from seasonal average.
   - Increased migratory movement toward urban centers in Central Europe: 76.5% spike predicted by Q4 20XX.
3. **Global Level:**
   - Financial markets will see a sharp decline of 6.1% in composite indices on 2027-04-28 due to

unspecified geopolitical instability.
  ○ Emergence of new socio-religious group linked to "Body in the Sky" phenomenon: 88.9% likelihood of global media coverage by 20XX-06-10.

Uncertainty Flags:

- Regional gravitational anomalies linked to the Body's presence producing high-variance outcomes in predictive accuracy.
- Long-term ecological effects impacting variables outside model sensitivity parameters.

LET'S *begin by acknowledging the centrality of feasts and food in Jesus' ministry. The Gospel of Luke, in particular, paints a vivid picture of a Messiah who is "always eating and drinking." In Luke 7:34, Jesus explicitly states:*

"The Son of Man has come eating and drinking, and you say, 'Here is a glutton and a drunkard, a friend of tax collectors and sinners.'"

This accusation from his opponents reflects a pattern in his life. Unlike John the Baptist, who adopted an ascetic lifestyle, Jesus engaged deeply with the social construct of his community, often in the context of shared meals. Feasting was not a side note; it was central to his ministry.

The first miracle of Jesus recorded in the Gospel of John is profoundly symbolic: turning water into wine at a wedding in Cana (John 2:1–11). This event was a celebration of abundance and joy. Weddings in first-century Jewish culture were multi-day festivities, and running out of wine would have been a significant embarrassment. Jesus' choice to intervene, and his provision of wine in extraordinary quality and quantity, signals endorsement of celebration.

Unlike feeding the five thousand, where hunger was the issue, the wedding at Cana highlights Jesus' attention to the importance of community joy and festivity. His action suggests that celebrating life and relationships should be considered a sacred act.

Throughout the Gospels, Jesus repeatedly dines with individuals considered outcasts and sinners: tax collectors, prostitutes, and the socially maligned. Consider the story of Levi, a tax collector whom Jesus calls in Luke 5:27–32. After this, Levi holds a great banquet, and Jesus attends, dining alongside tax collectors and others considered undesirable by religious authorities.

The Pharisees grumble:

"Why do you eat and drink with tax collectors and sinners?" (Luke 5:30).

Jesus' response is both profound and revealing:

"It is not the healthy who need a doctor, but the sick. I have not come to call the righteous, but sinners to repentance."

We see that meals are not just about food—they are transformative events where Jesus demonstrates the inclusivity of God's love. The table becomes a space of healing and reconciliation, but it is also a space of enjoyment and laughter.

The Kingdom of God, as described in the parables, is often compared to a feast or banquet. In Luke 14:15–24, Jesus tells the Parable of the Great Banquet, where the master invites the poor, the crippled, the blind, and the lame to his table after the originally invited guests refuse to come. This imagery underscores the joy, abundance, and inclusivity of God's reign.

These parables reinforce the idea that celebration is not frivolous but foundational to understanding the divine. Feasting is a metaphor for the communion between humanity and God—a vision of a world where everyone has a seat at the table, regardless of social or moral status.

The significance of wine cannot be overstated. Wine is a recurring symbol, symbolizing joy, abundance, and the new covenant. Consider the Last Supper, where Jesus uses wine to represent his blood, shed for the forgiveness of sins (Matthew 26:27–29). While this is a deeply solemn moment, it also parallels the celebratory nature of feasting— Jesus reframes the Passover meal to establish a new covenant based in communal sharing.

The fact that Jesus participated in wine-drinking and what we would consider parties suggests that he embraced the cultural norms of celebration, using them to convey profound theological truths. It is no coincidence that wine, associated with festivity, becomes a central symbol of his message.

Finally, we must recognize that joy and celebration are intrinsic to Jesus' understanding of the Kingdom of God. In John 15:11, Jesus says:

"I have told you this so that my joy may be in you and that your joy may be complete."

Jesus embodied a joy that invited others to participate. His feasts, his miracles at weddings, and his gatherings with outcasts all point to a theology of joy—one that sees laughter, music, and food as holy expressions of God's presence.

Jesus as a "party animal" might seem like a provocation, but it aligns with the Gospel accounts of his life and ministry. He was not afraid to engage with the social aspects of human life. Feasting, far from being frivolous, became a space for teaching, healing, and modeling the Kingdom of God.

Let us not ignore this aspect of Jesus: the one who turned water into wine, dined with outcasts, and proclaimed a Kingdom of joy and abundance. In embracing the human experience fully, Jesus invites us to celebrate life and share it with others.

Some of the class laughed. He could hear huffs as he gave the lecture, undoubtedly coming from John. It would likely be the cause of another complaint. Mrs Peters would assuredly react the same way if he was to deliver it on a Sunday morning.

———

As the days turned to weeks, more people came to where the man had stopped.

With them they brought their belongings and shelter. The people would stop and watch the sky. They would watch the sky as long as their bodies would allow them before they reached collapse. At the point where their body would give out, muscles atrophying, limbs weak, their eyes burning with visions of the world overhead they could not look away from, others would come and fill their place, still others would soothe them and notice the ecstatic look on their faces and the tears of joy that rolled down their cheeks. Some would convulse, an unheard rhythm coursing through their bodies. They would be given water and shelter.

People brought tents and created a village that provided the support that those watching needed to sustain their vigil.

At the centre of the people, the man stood still and continued his watch. All ensured that his space was never filled when he needed to retire and rejuvenate for his next time.

He no longer spoke. The few that he had spoken to all those days ago were blessed that he had told them they were watched and then had ceased speaking.

Despite this, the people knew what he wished of them in their hushed communion. And so they basked in the gaze of the power that resided in the sky.

As the weeks turned to months, the people took up residence in the park. The trees slowly coming back to life following the unexpectedly frigid winter. They had lost some during the days of the snowfalls. The old, the infirm, that could not take the exposure.

The people saw them as weak. The man never said as much but they knew.

The townsfolk were restless. They had lost people to the hill where they watched. There was a tension running through the town. At first, those with shops had welcomed the visitors, bringing people from out of town, selling more than they normally would. As time went on, the people in town started to grow angry with the people on the hill. The council went to visit them but still the man wouldn't speak and the people on the hill told them they were hurting no one and doing nothing wrong.

Law enforcement would come to believe that the numbers on the hill were growing through private chat rooms on the internet. Nothing else explained the way the numbers grew when the people barely spoke and spent their days staring at the sky.

Such groups began to pop up in other areas across the globe. Where they would be found was seemingly random but always the people would stare at the sky and do little else while the number of people would swell around them. Some towns would become ghosts, haunted by its former residents who now spent their time bathing in the gaze of the body that hung mute in the sky.

Still the man did not speak. When it came time for him to vacate his spot on the hill, his limbs raw, his eyes burning, he would make his way to a tent that others had erected for him. On occasion he would entwine himself with one of his flock, his hushed moans barely escaping the tent. At other times, he would go into a frenzy and write for hours, words tumbling out of him unbidden, unwanted, not within his control, furious muses taking over his cramped fingers and spewing forth apocalyptic visions of the future, bathed in fire, bathed in fire.

Law enforcement readied themselves.

ANNA WAS STILL SLEEPING SOFTLY when he woke. He gazed at her for a time, the morning light coming in at an angle that rested on her face, bathing her in a halo.

He sighed and rose. He thought he could hear Lisa in her room but it could be a fox outside.

Running through the fresh air of the morning, he pushed his legs to go faster, faster, he wasn't going to break down the way his father had. The sound of his heart and lungs filled his ears. The crunch of his shoes on the road punctuating.

The church looked lonely as he came up the hill. The stark

background of the sky framing the weathered building, all alone on the hill.

He showered and checked the vegetable patch out the back of the building. Mrs Peters had been out there earlier in the week. He had seen her out the window. He couldn't deal with her then, the never ceasing stream of consciousness drivel that she worked herself into when there was no one else that she knew would take his focus.

The tomato plants were blooming, despite the cold spell they had suffered through, the effects of the Body apparently. Mrs Peters had clearly harvested. Fat, deep red tomatoes that he knew were excellent. She may be a thorn in his side but she knew her way around a garden and without a doubt her produce would have won awards back when the church community was alive and had things like fairs and other fundraising events that would bring everyone together and people would receive prizes and Mrs Peters would be among them and her tomatoes would be purchased and people would tell her how blessed she was to have such a way in a garden that it was a God given talent.

I know these are confusing times. I know many of you look to the Body in the sky and see answers — or, perhaps, you see nothing but more questions. Some have left here, seeking certainty elsewhere, hoping to find the assurance that I cannot give you. And I understand that. Certainty is a comforting thing. It wraps around us like a warm blanket, shields us from the chill of doubt.

David hastily scratched out the words. He was at a loss at what to say.

He wandered up and down the length of the church. HIs focus moved over the state of the pews, the faded stain glass windows, the worn lectern. His father had told him this is what he would do when he found the words out of his grasp.

Distract yourself to become a vessel, he would say. The words are there, you just need to not look for them, he would say.

David's mind wandered to the call from church office. They knew attendance was down. They knew the collection was light. They were saying they would need to replace him. The church didn't look like much but it was valuable real estate in church office's portfolio which they would happily divest themselves of if someone didn't start having a full house on a Sunday morning. It wasn't enough to run a depressing Narc Anon meeting twice a week and look to let the local community group hold meetings there once a month, he would need to find a way to get people in. Doug would be able to pack the place. Doug would never consider the place because it was far too small and spoke to a type of Christian that Doug had little time for.

~~I don't know what the Body is. I don't know if it's a sign, a warning, or just... a mystery. And I won't stand here and pretend to know. But I do know this: How we respond to it, how we respond to each other in these times, matters. The world doesn't need more certainty; it needs more compassion. It needs more listening. It needs more love.~~

David stopped in the middle of the church, his feet heavy on the worn carpet running the length of the building.

He looked at the image of Jesus on the wall behind the lectern.

- Where have you gone?

He wasn't expecting a response.

- You were there and now you're not. Where have you gone?

He could feel anger building up in him.

- I used to hear you, I swear I used to hear you and now you just aren't here anymore. Nothing. Absolute silence. I could feel you, it wasn't the experience that idiots like Doug call it but I could feel that you were there. Then you just stopped.

He drew breath, ready to spew forth more words but they caught in his throat, refusing to come out, not knowing what he could say or what he was doing.

- Fuck you! Fuck you! Fuck you!

He grabbed a prayer book tucked into the back of one of the pews and hurled it at the image. It bounced off with a thud, leaving no mark.

His body felt like it was ready to explode, all raw nerves and tangled thoughts.

Mrs. Peters' quiet voice made him turn with a start. His shoulders slumped and he wondered how long she had been standing there. Her face was a mask of disappointment.

- Pastor Hale.

- Mrs. Peters. Good morning. How are you?

- I'm… what are you doing? I'm not early am I?

- No, no. I'm fine. I'm just preparing for the service.

- I see.

They stared at one another for a moment, each one not sure how to break the strange tension hanging between them.

- I… I picked some tomatoes earlier in the week. I was wondering if you and Anna would like some of them? I've kept some aside at home in case you do. They're quite delicious. You are welcome to as many as you would like. I'm sure that Anna would be able to cook you a special dinner with them.

- Thank you. Maybe. I'm not sure.

- Well please do let me know. I guess I'll go and take my seat for the service. Are you expecting many people to come today?

David felt the rage start to crawl up his throat again.

- What are you even doing here?

- I'm sorry, Pastor Hale, I'm not sure what you mean.

- You can see that there's no one else here. You can see that right?

- Well, yes, I...

- You're the only one who keeps on coming, everyone else has stopped.

- I do know that Mr Runnels and Mrs. Walton have started going to Pastor Jenkins church, yes. They talked to me about it. I admit I went to a sermon there last Thursday. I didn't think much of it. Too many people, too much theatre and drama, it was like going to Catholic mass. No, definitely not for me. This is the church I go to. I much prefer your sermons, Pastor Hale.

- Why? Why on earth would you want my sermons? What do you want from me? Why? There's nothing left. No people. There is nothing left here.

- Because this is the church I go to.

- There are other churches. It doesn't have to be Doug's church but there are other places.

- No, Pastor Hale, there aren't. This is the church I go to. This is the church I got married in. Your father married me and my husband, Edward. Right here. This is where I come on Sunday mornings. This is where I used to come with Edward. We loved your father. I know you aren't the preacher he was, he could hold a room but you mean well and you are your own man and you feel God, I know you do.

- It isn't enough.

- Of course it is. Even if you leave and no one else ever comes, I'll still come and tend to the garden and sit here in prayer. This is the place I feel my Edward more than anywhere else, and I will never let that go.

Mrs. Peters' face looked tangled with sorrow and nerves.

She looked to say something more but then turned and walked out of the church.

David stayed, unmoving, until he was sure that she was outside.

ABOUT THE AUTHOR

Sean Mackaay writes a lot. Always has. It keeps coming back to the apocalypse, he's never sure why. He wonders if he never managed to properly get over *Absolution* by Muse.

You can often find him at THE AUTHOR IS DUMB, reviewing movies and TV shows, and dropping his new books in instalments. You can send him all your questions there.

ALSO BY SEAN MACKAAY

Endless Cycle

Pattern Machine

Lunch Eater

www.ingramcontent.com/pod-product-compliance
Lightning Source LLC
Chambersburg PA
CBHW030416120726
47904CB00007B/2297